Trophy Husband

by Lauren Blakely

Table of Contents

<u>Contact</u>

Also by Lauren Blakely

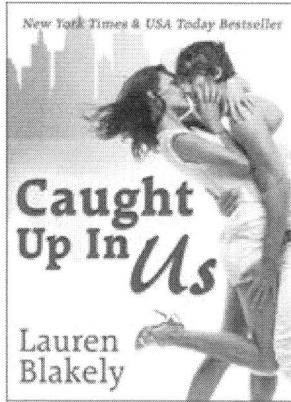

Caught Up In Us
Available at all fine e-tailers

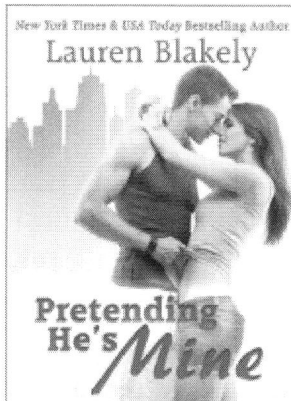

Pretending He's Mine
Available at all fine e-tailers

About

Sometimes you can't help falling in love, even when you try to do the opposite...Successful fashion blogger McKenna Bell has spent far too long protecting herself after the way her ex-fiancé left her at the altar for a college chick he met the night of his bachelor party. Loving again, trusting again, well, that's just not in the cards. Especially now that her ex is back in town with his new woman, demanding custody of McKenna's favorite creature in the whole world--her dog. No effing way. McKenna's had enough of him, and she decides to even the score by finding her own hot young thing -- a Trophy Husband. Sure, she's only twenty-seven, but doesn't that make it even more fun -- and infuriating to her ex -- to pursue a younger man? When she declares her intentions on her daily blog, her quest quickly skyrockets in popularity, and that's when Chris enters the picture, and he's got all the assets. He's handsome, successful, and turns her inside out with a kiss to end all kisses, the kind that makes you feel like a shooting star. But loving again could mean losing again, and it's so much easier to focus on getting even, isn't it? Unless, you just can't help falling in love. Which means McKenna will have to come face to face with what she really wants in life -- protecting her heart from hurt, or letting go of her fears of a new beginning.

Dedication

This book is dedicated to my family.
Because they put up with me, and I love them madly.

Prologue

Present Day

The stars twinkle and the night air is warm as we leave the Tiki Bar and walk slowly up Fillmore. At the top of the hill, I see my friend's maroon Prius that I'm tasked with driving home tonight. I point to it.

"These are my wheels." I click on the key to unlock the car. Then I reach for the door handle. But it doesn't open. I try again. Same thing happens. "Damn. What is up with these hybrids?"

"They have to calibrate to your heart rate."

"Then how the heck am I supposed to drive it home?"

"I know a trick," Chris says.

"You do?"

"Want to give me the keys and I'll show you?" he asks, holding open his palm for me.

But before I can pull away, he closes his fingers over mine, gripping my hand in his. That's all it takes. Within seconds I am in his arms, and we are wrapped up in each other. His lips are sweeping mine, and I press my hands against his chest, and oh my. He does have the most fantastic outlines in his body. He is toned everywhere, strong everywhere, and I am dying to get my hands up his shirt, and feel his bare chest and his belly. But if I did, I might just jump him right here because I am one year and running

9

without this. Without kissing, without touching, without feeling this kind of heat.

He twines his fingers through my hair, and the way he holds me, both tender and full of want at the same time, makes me start to believe in possibilities. Start to believe that you can try again, and it'll be worth it. His lips are so soft, so unbearably soft, and I can't stop kissing him. He has the faintest taste of Diet Coke on his lips, and it's crazy to say this, but it almost makes me feel closer to him. Or maybe I feel closer because he's leaning into me, his body is aligned with mine, and there's no space between us, and I don't want any space between us. I want to feel him against me, his long, strong body tangled up in mine, even though we're fully clothed, making out on the street.

He breaks the kiss. "I wanted to kiss you all night."

"You did?"

"Yeah, that key thing was just an excuse. Sometimes you just have to hit the button a few times to get the car to open."

I laugh. "So you said that to kiss me?"

He nods. "Totally."

"I'm glad you tricked me," I whisper, as he bends his head and kisses my neck, blazing a trail of sweet and sexy kisses down to my throat, and it's almost sensory overload the way he ignites me. Forget tingles, forget goosebumps. That's kid stuff compared to this. My body is a comet with Chris. I am a shooting star with the way he kisses me. I don't even know if I have bones in my body anymore. I don't know how I'm standing. I could melt under the sweet heat of his lips that are now tracing a line down my chest to the very top of my breasts as he tugs gently at my shirt, giving himself room to leave one more brush of his lips. Before he stops.

He looks at me and the expression on his face is one of pride and lust. He knows he's turned me inside out and all the way on.

"That was so unfair of me," he says with a wicked grin. "Getting a headstart like that on all the other candidates."

How can there be any other guys after a kiss like that? It's a kiss to end all kisses, it's a sip of lemonade in a hammock on a warm summer day. It's a slow dance on hardwood floors while a fan goes round overhead, curtains blowing gently in the open window.

If he feels half as much for me as I do for him, then I want to sail away with him in the moonlight, and that scares the hell out of me. I have to extract myself before I let this go any further. I don't mean the contact. I mean the way my aching, broken heart is reaching for Chris.

Chapter One

Four weeks ago…

I used to have sucky parking karma, the kind where every single time I needed a spot, and especially if I was racing to a lunch meeting, the only one I could locate would be in the next county, and in some cases, the next time zone.

Then one year ago, a miracle occurred. No, my ex-boyfriend didn't fall back in love with me and announce it was all a joke when he eloped with some chick in Vegas at his bachelor party the night before our wedding. But another miracle transpired. Since then I have never failed to land a parking spot on the same block as my destination. I am quite sure this is the universe's way of making up for precisely how he said sayonara – via voicemail mere hours before I was about to walk down the aisle.

And because of this awesome, amazing, powerful parking karma I no longer worry that I'll drive around scouting out a spot in the city of San Francisco, even though time in this city can truly be measured by the quest for a parking spot.

One less thing to stress about is a good thing in my book, so I give my gorgeous dog, Ms. Pac-Man, a kiss on the snout as I grab my purse from the entryway table. She wags her flag-sized, blond fluffy tail and places a big paw on my leg, her way of saying goodbye. She's a good dog, she's well-trained, and she's also particularly well-mannered when I leave her home alone in the Victorian she and I share just a few blocks from San Francisco Bay. She spends the entire time I'm gone snoozing on her Pac-Man decorated dog bed. I know this because I once set up my phone camera to verify what I suspected – that she was indeed a perfect canine.

"I'd tell you to be good, but I know you will," I say, as I scratch her ears. She leans her soft head into my hand, and I smile as I pet her. Sometimes, I think this dog is the only reason I've smiled at all in the last year. Not much has made me happy, but yet here she is, ably filling that role as only a dog can.

Then I'm off to another solo Sunday breakfast, heading down the stairs, to the garage, into the car, and onto the street, driving past a local grocery store where bag boys fill canvas sacks with organic chickens, locally-grown asparagus and all-natural, wheat-free cereals, then a membership-only nail salon that I don't go to. Because I do my own nails, in alternating colors, and today I am wearing mint green and purple.

I turn the radio up louder, and even though I should listen to angry girl rock given how my heart's been in a sling for the last year, I can't bring myself to like that kind of music. Because deep down I am still the old standards I love. So I sing along to the music – Frank Sinatra's *I've Got You Under My Skin* – as I motor up steep hills that burn legs while walking, then down a rollercoaster-y dip on my way into Hayes Valley. The station shifts to the King, another favorite of this retro-loving girl, and he's now crooning *Can't Help Falling in Love*.

My favorite song ever.

The song Todd didn't want to be our wedding song since he'd insisted on *Have I Told You Lately That I Love You*, the perfect tune since that's how he felt about me, he claimed.

A red Honda scoots out of the prime spot right in front of the restaurant. As I glide my orange Mini Cooper into the space, I mouth a silent thank you to the parking gods. Don't get me wrong – I'm grateful for the way they look out for me and reward me with perfect little nooks for my car, but I have other daydreams too.

Yet those ones seem so far out of reach.

Mainly, I'd like to find a guy who's not a weasel. The kind of fella who doesn't ring you up from Sin City to call the whole thing off the day before you're supposed to slip into a gorgeous white dress with that perfect '50s flair you were looking for.

"Listen, I've had a change of heart," Todd said on my voice mail because I was on another call with the cake shop. It would have been a perfect wedding. We had what I thought was a perfect life. Cramped but cozy apartment in the Mission, my business was taking off like crazy and he'd helped launch it, we'd even picked out names for kids we might have some day – Charlotte for a girl and Hunter for a boy.

Then he had an epiphany at a poker table in Vegas when he met a gymnast he married instead.

The day before our wedding.

"I don't really see myself having kids with you, or a life with you, so let's nip this thing in the bud," he said in his phone message.

So yeah. That kind of sucked.

But as I listen to this song, I find myself longing for something more in my life. For someone to join me for breakfast at my favorite diner in the city. Maybe a sweet kiss, a nice goodnight make-out session, and maybe some love too, the kind of love that lasts, always and forever, without leaving you in the lurch, I admit silently, as Elvis croons about taking my hand and my whole heart too.

Why do I do this? Why do I listen to this music that tortures me? I thought my almost-hubs and I were meant to be, and I was wrong, but yet as The King sings about falling in love, I can't deny that there's a part of me that wouldn't mind falling in love again.

The kind where you can't help it.

The kind that takes your breath away.

The kind that's meant to be.

I know, I know. It's like asking for the moon, so I'll stop my silly daydreaming.

But, hey, at least right now I have a coveted parking spot.

I snatch my purse with its saucy cartoon of a winking pirate girl on the side and head into The Best Doughnut Shop in the City. It's not really a doughnut shop. It used to be a doughnut shop and then the owner converted it into a diner with green upholstered vinyl seats. It's my absolute favorite diner in the whole city and it feels a bit like my special place.

I tell the hostess I'm a party of one, and look, I'm not going to lie – it still hurts to ask for that solo table, even though Todd never once, in all our five years together, came with me to this diner. He said he didn't care for cheap, hole-in-the-wall eateries. Snob.

But even when I came here all by myself for Sunday breakfast, at least I was still part of a two-some, even if the other someone was sleeping in. Now, it's just me. Party of one.

I keep my chin up as the hostess guides me to one of the last remaining two-tops. The place is packed. *See Todd? You don't know what you were missing. This cheap diner knows how to bring it in the breakfast department.*

I sit down and smooth out my flouncy knee-length poodle skirt. Even if I'm all by my lonesome, I still like to dress up. Fashion is like a shield to me. The clothes I wear center me, make me strong and steely with their distinctive style.

I order my usual – scrambled eggs, toast and a Diet Coke. Yep, I'm one of those people who drinks soda in the mornings. I'm sure I should kick the habit for many reasons, including the fact that Todd was my Diet Coke partner in crime, and we both downed the carbonated beverage morning, noon and night. But I refuse to let the memory of what we shared ruin my favorite drink.

One minute later the waitress brings me a glass that's fizzing just the right amount. I thank her and take a drink, then reach for my laptop from my bag. I might as well work on my fashion blog as I wait for the food. As I flip open the computer, the waitress guides a gorgeous young redhead over to the two-top next to me. I scan her outfit first. The gal is wearing sparkling white running shoes with a pink swirly stripe, black workout pants and a color-coordinated snug workout top. There's something about her face though that's eerily familiar. Like I've seen her somewhere, but I can't place it.

She flashes me a warm smile. "Hi," she says.

"Hey."

"This placed is jammed today."

"It's like this every Sunday. The food is amazing."

"I've heard great things about it. I'm so excited to finally try it."

Okay, maybe I won't need the laptop. Maybe this gal and I will chat for the next thirty minutes, seeing as she's mighty friendly. I wouldn't mind the company, to tell the truth. It beats eating over a keyboard. "You will not be disappointed. Everything's good."

"My husband said he's been wanting to go to this place for the longest time. He's just out parking the car," she says and tips her forehead to the door.

I half expected her to say her dad was going to join her because she looks like a teenager. But maybe she was a teenage bride. "Well, both of you will love it then. I'm a total regular. A *devotee*, as they say." I add in a silly little affected accent that makes her laugh.

"What do you recommend?"

"Anything. Except for hard-boiled eggs, because they're totally gross."

"Oh god, yes. They're like the most disgusting food ever."

I lean closer and say in a conspiratorial whisper. "My ex used to love them. I couldn't even be in the house when he ate hard-boiled eggs."

"You want to hear something funny? My husband used to love them too. But I laid down the law. No hard-boiled eggs ever in my house. I cured him of his hard-boiled egg addiction like that." She snaps her fingers.

I hold up a hand to high five her. "You deserve major points."

"Oh, look. There he is," she says, and when I turn to follow her gaze, it's as if I've had a pair of cleats jammed into my belly, and I don't even play softball. But I bet this is what it feels like when the batter slides into home and you're the catcher who's not wearing a chest protector.

Blindsided.

Because she's looking at Todd.

The diner is shrinking. The walls are closing in, gripping me. I can't breathe. This has to be a mistake. An error. She has to be joking. I have to be seeing things. There is no way her husband can be Todd. There must be another man behind him, maybe a short man I can't see. A pipsqueak little fellow right behind Todd, who's walking over to her table. But there's no mini man hiding behind him. It's just him, and he freezes when he sees me, then quickly recovers, taking the seat across from his wife.

Wife.

It's as if there's a knife in my heart, digging for all the soft spots and scooping them out. Serving them up on the table for the two of them. The girl-child I've been chatting with, my new fucking breakfast best friend, is the college-age creature from Vegas who stole my about-to-be-husband.

I've never seen her in person before. I have only seen one photo I found of her on Facebook the day after his voicemail, as I sobbed and clicked, surrounded by unopened wedding gifts sent to our apartment. Now I feel stupid for not studying her photos more, for not hunting out more pictures of her online. I stopped after that one – a faraway shot of her at a gymnastics meet since, of course, she's a gymnast – because it hurt far too much. But now with her here in front of me, I catalogue her features. Her cheeks are rosy, her skin is soft and smooth, her hair is auburn red and shampoo model bouncy with perfect waves, and her boobs remind me of Salma Hayek's.

They're so freaking huge.

Fine, I'm only six years older, but I have straight brown hair that I color blond, and weird eyes that are sometimes blue, sometimes green, sometimes gray, and my breasts are decent, but not dead ringers for cantaloupes. I'm only twenty-seven and I know it sucks to be left at any age. But the fact that he left me for a co-ed – giving himself a trophy wife for all intents and purposes – didn't help my self-esteem. I'd been with him for five years; she'd been with him for one night, and she got him all the way to the altar. I got stuck with two mixers I never use, and *party-of-one* as my middle name.

"Hi McKenna," Todd says in his best business-like voice.

"Oh…." It's like a long, slow release of air from Amber, as her mouth drops open, and she shifts her gaze from him to me, registering who she's been chatting with.

She recovers faster than me though, because I'm still speechless and stuck in this chair, sitting next to Amber. She is the name of all my heartbreak. The name that drummed through my brain for the

18

better part of the last twelve months, like an insistent hum in the pipes you can't turn off. *Amber, Amber, Amber.* The woman he wanted. The woman he chose. I will never hear that name without thinking of all that she has that I don't. The man I once wanted to marry.

"You know, why don't we just get a new table?" she says to Todd.

He scans the restaurant. This is the last empty table. "There's no place else to sit," he says, and it's clear he has no intention of leaving.

What's also clear is that he's the only of us – him and me – who doesn't care that he ran into his ex-fiancé. That realization smacks me hard, but it reminds me that I need to pull myself together and channel whatever reserves of steely coolness I have in me.

"It's fine. I'm almost done anyway," I manage to say even though my food hasn't arrived.

"So how's everything going with you?" He reaches for a menu and scans it. He doesn't even look at me while he's talking. It's not because he's rude. It's because I am nothing to him. There's a stinging feeling in the back of my eyes. I tighten my jaw. I won't let them see me cry.

"Great. The blog is great. The dog is great. Life is great," I say, pretending I am a robot, an unfeeling robot who can spit out platitudes. I have to. I have to protect my heart because it feels like it's being filleted. "I see you like this place now?"

"I love it. Favorite diner in the whole city."

My throat catches, and I grit my teeth. "That's great. And such great news about the hard-boiled eggs too."

He gives me a curious look.

"Nothing. It's nothing." I affix a plastic smile when the waitress brings me my food. She turns to Todd and Amber. They order as I slide my laptop into my bag and consider ditching the place right now. Who needs food when there are ex-fiancés and their new wives to remind you of all that was stolen from you?

"And I'll have a coffee too. No more soda in the morning for me," he adds before the waitress leaves.

The burning behind my eyes intensifies. *It's just coffee,* I tell myself. But he used to *hate* coffee. He detested it, and now he's drinking it instead of Diet Coke.

He turns his attention back to Amber. "But no coffee for you still," he says to her in a babyish voice. She smiles at Todd as he lays a hand gently on one of hers. I try my hardest to mask the all-too familiar feeling of my insides being shred by him. God, I loved this man. I was a fool, but I loved him like crazy, I fell for him the day I met him randomly at a bus stop several years ago. He was mine, and he was wonderful, and he was the only one I wanted.

"Well, it was great seeing you," I say, and start to push my chair away.

"You're leaving?"

"Yeah. I totally forgot that I ate a bagel already today. Stupid me." I smack my forehead, as if I'm shocked at my own forgetfulness.

"I do that sometimes too," Amber says. "Forget stuff. I think it's because I have baby brain right now."

"Excuse me?"

"Oh," she says, and there it is again. That long expression of surprise.

Todd nods several times. "We had a baby. Two weeks ago."

My heart races into a very painful overdrive of disbelief as it pounds against my chest. This can't be happening. Todd clasps his hand over Amber's and she beams at him, and that smile, for her, just for her, threatens my precarious sense of *I'm-totally-fine-with-being-ditched-the-day-before-our-wedding.*

"We have a little sweet little baby girl. Her name is Charlotte."

The diner starts spinning and I grab the edge of the table. I squeeze my eyes shut, hoping, praying that'll do the trick and hold in the tears that are threatening to splash all over my face. He changed everything for her, all the way from children to breakfast choices. And he took everything from me, including our name for a baby he wound up having a year after leaving me a voicemail that said he didn't want to marry me because he couldn't picture having kids with me.

I open my eyes. Take a deep breath. Try to keep it together. "That was our name."

"It's a beautiful name too," Amber says. "She's such a beautiful baby, and so smart too. She's with my parents right now over in Marin. But I miss her and I've only been away from her for an hour."

"We're madly in love with being parents," he adds.

That does it. He might have cut out my heart with an Exacto blade, but I won't let him know it's bleeding again. I have to get away from them.

"You should really get back to her then," I somehow manage to choke out as I stand up and grab my bag, doing everything not to trip and fall as I leave my food on the table, and rush to the restroom, where I slam the stall door and let the tears rain down. My shoulders shake, my chests heaves, and I am sure I look like a wretched mess. After several minutes, I check the time. But I know they're still out there, so I stay inside this stall as other patrons come and go. I camp out in the safety behind this door, registering each minute.

Until an hour passes.

Then I unlock the stall, splash water on my face, and touch up my mascara and blush.

I don't feel human, but I can at least pass for one again. I open the door a crack, spotting the table where he delivered his latest crushing blow. I thought I was over him. I thought I couldn't be more over him. But seeing him with her reopened everything I thought I'd gotten over by playing Call of Duty and shooting bad guys every night for the last several months.

I head for the counter, pay the hostess for the food I didn't eat, and then I leave The Best Doughnut Shop in The City. Another wave of sadness smashes into me when I realize I'll never be able to come to my favorite diner again. He's ruined this place for me.

I'm so ready to go home and curl up with Ms. Pac-Man for a bit, so I hurry over to my car, where I see a white piece of paper tucked under the wiper, flapping in the wind. Now I have a parking ticket? Now my karma bites me in the back? No, this should be the day when I find a winning lottery ticket on my car, not a parking ticket.

I turn around to peer up at the sign. The white and red sign very clearly says Sunday mornings are free. I glance at the curb. It's not red. There's no hydrant nearby. I scan the block. Down near the corner of Hayes Street, I see the meter boy, wearing his uniform of blue shorts and a blue short-sleeved button-down shirt. I grab the parking ticket and march down the street to confront him.

He's slipping another ticket under the windshield of a lime-green Prius. "What's up with the ticket?"

He turns around to face me and I feel like I've been blinded. He is shatteringly good-looking. His face is chiseled, his light blue eyes sparkle, his brown hair looks amazingly soft. I can't help but give him a quick perusal up and down. It's clear he is completely sculpted underneath his parking attendant uniform. Every single freaking inch of him. He smiles at me, straight white teeth gleaming back. He's so beautiful, my eyes hurt. It's like looking at the sun.

My ticket rage melts instantly. My resolve turns into a puddle.

"Oh, hi. I saw you earlier when you parked."

"You did?"

He's smiling at me, giving me some sort of knowing grin that unnerves me. He's probably all of twenty-one, just like Amber. He does not possess the tire that the men I see – at the coffee shops or dog parks – wear around their midsections. No, this fellow owns a pair of noticeably cut biceps and an undeniably trim waist. Why have I not spent more time hanging around the meters in this city with its bevy of beautiful, young, sexy parking attendants?

"Hey, I've got some other cars to deal with. But call me later." Then he winks at me. He crosses the street.

"I didn't park illegally," I shout at him.

He smiles again, that radiant smile still strong from across the street. "I know."

I stand there for a moment, befuddled on the corner of the street. *Call me,* he said. How would I call him? I look at the ticket in my hand and flip it over.

There is no check mark on it, no official signature, no indication of a parking crime. Instead, there's a a simple note: "You're gorgeous. Give me a call sometime." Then there's a number.

I shake my head. I'm floored by the turn of events. By the shift in my day from utter crap to a pick-up line. *Okay, McKenna – which is more implausible? That your ex-fiancé had a baby with her? Or that an achingly handsome young meter man wants you to call him for a date?*

I walk slowly back to my car, still in a daze. I reach my Mini Cooper and lean against my car for just a minute, not caring if the backside of my sky blue skirt picks up dirt – a skirt I snagged when my girlfriends Hayden and Erin stole me away for a wine country spa weekend to forget all my woes, and it didn't work, but I did score some cute clothes at a vintage shop I found next to a bowling alley on the drive home. I flip the ticket over again, looking at Meter Man's number. Then I glance one more time down the street and see him on the other side now, writing out parking tickets. He must feel my faraway eyes on him, because he looks up and waves at me. He mimics the universal sign for *phone*, holding up his hand against his ear, thumb and pinky out. I can't help myself. I laugh at the incredulity of this all. I read the note yet another time. *"You're gorgeous. Call me."*

There's a part of me that wants to lock myself inside and have a pity party. To call my girlfriends and let them help me drown my sorrows as they have done every single time I've needed them to in the last year. But if Todd can change everything about himself, maybe I can too. So I go against my natural instinct to retreat. Instead, I pull my phone from my purse and dial the meter man's number. I watch him off in the distance as he extracts his phone from his pocket.

"I'm glad you didn't make me wait."

Be still my beating heart. He's hot, he's nice and he's flirty.

"I'm glad I didn't wait either. So, what's your name?"

"Dave Dybdahl."

I try not to laugh at the odd alliteration of his double-D – wait, make that *triple-D* – sounding name.

"Dave, why'd you leave this note for real? You're not trying to pull a joke on me and I'm really going to have some massive parking fine?"

He laughs, then assumes a very serious voice. "I never joke about parking meter matters," he says and I'm liking that he's got a little sense of humor working underneath that fine exterior. "I saw you get out of your car before you went into the diner and I thought you were pretty. Want to go out sometime?"

I laugh again. A date. I don't have dates. I have shooting sessions with video games. I have crying fests with my girlfriends. I share a king-size bed with a lab-hound-husky.

And I have a hope that it all may change. That this life of the last year is not my life to come. That this day is the nail in the coffin on my heartbreak. That the songs I listen to could someday be sung for me. The ones about mad, crazy, never-gonna-let-you-go love. Maybe with Dave Dybdahl. Maybe with someone else.

"Why not? I'll call you later to make a plan."

"I can't wait."

I hang up the phone and stare at it again, still not sure if that conversation really just happened. I push the phone back into my bag and it suddenly occurs to me that Todd doesn't have to be the only one who gets to win here. I am single, I have a good job, an awesome job in fact, and I'm not bad looking.

Todd took my heart. He took my name. He took himself. He gave it all to Amber, his Trophy Wife. But that moment in the Best Doughnut Shop in the City doesn't have to be the last word, does it? He doesn't deserve any more tears. He doesn't deserve any more of my pain. There is no more room for sadness or hurt.

I have to move on and I finally know how.

Because my brain has hatched the perfect plan, right here, right now, thanks to this handsome young meter man. I can turn the tables. I can even the score and take up the mantle for all the jilted ladies, young and old. This is no longer about me. There is something bigger at stake here. I have been presented with a rare opportunity. This isn't just happenstance. This isn't just coincidence.

This is real parking karma at work.

Because if the unbelievably hot Dave Dybdahl thinks I'm cute, then maybe, just maybe, I could land a hot young thing, a delicious piece of arm candy, a boy toy. Maybe Dave Dybdahl, maybe someone else. Because Dave will be just the beginning of my new project.

I am going to score myself a Trophy Husband.

Chapter Two

My next order of business is to convene a meeting with the brain trust.

So I scurry back to the Marina district where I live now. I got the hell out of our tiny little apartment in the Mission as soon as I could. One week after Todd had eloped with the Pretzel Gymnast, I'd packed up the whole place, thanks to help from my sister Julia and my good friend, Erin. She gets double helper points since she carried those frigging mixers, which are heavy bastards, all the way to Good Will by herself. Then I moved in with Julia for a few weeks as I looked for my own place, one that wasn't choked with memories of what I had thought was my big, epic, once-in-a-lifetime romance.

I found a new home fairly quickly, thanks in part to the sale of my video show, *The Fashion Hound*, to the media company Fashion Nation. I'm a matchmaker of outfits, hosting my own short daily show about where to find the coolest, funkiest, most unique looks, and how to pair them and *not* pair them together. *The Fashion Hound* took off online, and after several months Fashion Nation bought it and brought it into the fold. I still write and host the show.

The irony was the offer came in two weeks before the wedding. Todd and I even celebrated it together with a night out at a new restaurant in SoMa, and then dancing at a club, where we made out to the sounds of techno pop, and toasted to a big, fat payday for doing what I loved – video blogging about clothes.

Life couldn't have been better.

I had the guy, the gig, the dog, and the dough.

I still have the gig, the dog, and the dough, so I suppose three out of four ain't bad, and really, all things considered, *Don't Cry For Me Argentina.*

Even though, you know, my heart was pretty much severed.

But I love my job, and that's why I keep doing it every day, and besides the bigger house, I don't live off the money from the sale. I live off what I earn every day, though obviously I'm grateful for the financial padding. I know I'm lucky in business. I know I have a lot of things – my health, a house, and security. Not to mention, the world's most awesome dog. I wouldn't mind, though, being lucky in love. Alone at night, in my quiet home, in my king size bed, I miss company.

I miss music and laughter, and nights wrapped up with another person when that person feels like the world to you, and you to him. So maybe a hot young thing can be more than just a way to settle the score. Maybe a Trophy Husband would never leave me, never hurt me, never make me give up my favorite restaurant in the whole wide world. Maybe a Trophy Husband is precisely the kind of boy who could love a girl forever and ever and then some.

The kind of love that makes the crooners want to sing in sultry voices.

"But that's just between you and me, Ms. Pac-Man," I tell my dog as I curl up on the couch next to her and send an email to Julia, Hayden and Erin, letting them know their presence is required at my house this evening for an emergency meeting.

* * *

That night we switch the location to Hayden's house. She lives next door, which means we share a wall, an entryway, and a front stoop. Her husband, Greg, is out of town. They're both lawyers – he's a business attorney and she does patent law – and she's holed up in her home office, finishing a legal brief that's due for a client tomorrow, so I help her daughter Lena get ready for bed.

I adore her daughter for many reasons, including the fact that she loves clothes and fashion and is pretty much the best shopping partner ever. Sometimes, when Hayden and Greg need a break, I happily take Lena out for a girl's afternoon and we try on everything on Union Street. And I mean everything. The girl has power shopping genes twined deep in her DNA, and I love that kind of relentless-ness when it comes to clothing racks.

Lena waits for me at the end of the hall, pointing excitedly in her room. Lena's wavy brown hair is unkempt as usual, in desperate need of a brushing. But at eight years old, she's already learning some of the secret tricks of women. She has pushed it back with a red headband that's got big white polka dots on it. Very Marianne.

"By the way, I totally approve of the look," I say. "But your mom said we have to get you to bed. The girls are coming over soon."

"McKenna!" she shrieks, barely able to contain her excitement. "Look, look, look." She grabs my hand and pulls me into her room and begins stroking their Siamese cat Chaucer, who's curled around a stuffed teddy bear. Lena tucks her feet gracefully under her legs and keeps petting. She leans her face in to the cat, rubbing her cheek gently against his downy fur. "McKenna, do you think you can convince my mom to let him stay in the house tonight, just one night? You like animals, don't you?"

"Obviously."

"My mom doesn't like this cat, but he's making me so happy and I'll make sure he doesn't pee in the house. Please, please, please convince her."

The trouble with Chaucer is he's an equal opportunity whizzer. Hayden has told me all the stories of pet cleaning companies and furniture re-upholsterers she's called in to fix the damage this cat has done. But he's her husband's cat, and Greg is strangely crazy about him, so Hayden is forced to put up with Chaucer's predilection for pinpoint precise peeing. She manages by keeping the cat outside in their tiny backyard, which is adjacent to my very own tiny backyard.

"Lena, isn't he supposed to be in the backyard. Doesn't your mom want him outside?"

Lena buries her nose in his fur again.

"Lena," I say gently. "Did you let Chaucer in again?"

She doesn't look at me. She keeps Eskimo-kissing the cat. "I think he sneaked in. Um, it was when the Fedex guy dropped off that package at your doorstep."

"Ooh! That's my new tee-shirt for the show," I say, distracted momentarily from the cat's mode of entry. I've become known for cool and unusual tees, with interesting sayings, arty pictures, funky logos. I recently tracked down a tee-shirt from the online gift shop for the Metropolitan Opera – it's a black vee-neck tee-shirt and across the front in blood red it says "Macbeth," and toppling off the "h" is a crown. I can't wait to show it off in *The Fashion Hound.*

But I also enjoy the Fedex guy's visits for another reason. He's a certified babe. Yep, he's one of the many reasons I make sure to shower and apply make-up each morning because you never known when the Fedex man might need to make a delivery. Not *that* kind. Not yet, at least. He's totally hot, but I haven't quite figured out how to ask him out. I guess being out of the dating circuit for the last, oh, six years has handicapped me in this department. Even so, he's kind of become my sublimation, and the prospect of a visit from him is often enough to get me through the day.

"Do a fashion show for the girls, McKenna!" Lena leaps up from the bed, no longer interested in pleading Chaucer's cause. Instead, she's found a new one, all part of her strategy to delay bedtime.

Hayden's heels click down the hallway. "Bedtime for you, missy. Fashion show another time."

"No fashion show? That's blasphemy," I say to Hayden.

She shakes her head at me. "It's like having two kids sometimes."

Lena gives her mom a pout. "Can't I stay up and say hi to the ladies?"

"Nope."

Lena glances at her mom, then gives me a knowing smile. "You're letting Chaucer stay inside again!"

"Just for tonight," Hayden says, then she kisses her daughter and tucks her into bed. I head to the living room where I fiddle around with a new handheld camera I picked up the other day. I use a videographer for my show, but I like having my own small camera for little. odds and ends that I need to shoot on my own. Soon, Hayden finishes with Lena, leaving the cat in her room. "I don't have the heart to throw him back out. Not when Lena worked so hard to sneak him in and devise a cover up. I know the cat didn't just slip inside. He was aided and abetted by my daughter."

"Resourceful kid."

"If he pees on her bed, I am going to be so pissed though."

I laugh at her choice of verbs as I leave my camera on her coffee table, and head into the kitchen to prepare snacks.

"Thank you for helping me get her ready for bed."

"Well, you can just pay me back whenever I need a patent attorney."

"Babysitting bartering for legal advice you'll never need? Sounds completely fair," Hayden says, loading up her arms with a cheese platter and olive plate. I grab a small candy dish, and we return to the living room.

The dish wobbles in my hands when I spot Chaucer on the coffee table leaving his mark on my new camera. "Your cat!"

"Chaucer!" Hayden shouts angrily and scoops the cat from the table. "I'm so sorry, I'm so sorry, I'm so sorry," she repeats over and over. She marches to the backdoor, and I march to the kitchen where I find cleaner and some paper towels and try to rid my beautiful new handheld of that awful scent. I breathe in through my mouth as I clean, and once I'm done I try to turn on the camera. No luck. I shake my head at the cat, even though he's now outside where he belongs. But yet, I have to tip my hat to him. As much as Chaucer rankles me, in some perverse way I admire him. The deliberateness, the in-your-face-ness of his strategy. He hit me where it hurts and he didn't care. There's something about the sheer recklessness of him that I wish I had more of. The cat does what the cat wants, consequences be damned. I think I'm going to be like that cat. Not pee on cameras, of course. But, be bold. Be daring. Do what I want, no matter what.

Hayden apologizes twenty million more times. "I promise if you ever, ever, ever need a business attorney for anything, I will make Greg handle it for free."

"Let's just hope I never need a good business attorney, but if I do, I will gladly accept the blood money offer seeing as the dude who handled *The Fashion Hound* sale charged me two arms and three legs. Wait. Is that blood money? Or pee money?" I add with a wink.

But she doesn't respond. Instead, she bites her lip once, a sign that she wants to say something and is figuring out how.

"What? What is it, Hayden?"

"Are you sure you want to do this?"

"Do what?"

"You know what I mean. Look for a Trophy Husband."

"Yeah. Why wouldn't I?" I say, doing my best to be the tough guy I haven't been in a year.

"It just doesn't seem like you."

"Well, that's because this is the first time my ex-fiancé has told me he that he's had a baby with the woman he left me for, and took our baby name, to boot."

"I know, sweetie. And I know that hurts an insane amount," she says softly. "But…"

"But what?"

"But is this really going to help you get over him?"

Her question is a valid one, but try as I might to pack a full dose of toughness around my heart, the wound Todd inflicted is clearly still there. It hasn't closed. And nobody knows how much it still hurts as well as Hayden and my girls, who have been here for me, taking my late-night phone calls and rehashing every moment that led up to Todd's treacherous voicemail. They've tried to get me into yoga, they've sent me random hot guy of the day pictures, and they've engaged in more retail therapy than nearly anyone but a fashion blogger could handle. They've done everything to buoy me up, and it's very nearly worked.

But this morning sent me all the way back to start. I didn't pass go. I didn't collect two hundred dollars. So I need to find another way. This has to be the other way out of the heartbreak.

I throw my hands up in the air. "I don't know! Yes. No. Maybe. I mean, Hayden. I thought I was over him but seeing him today was a reminder that I'm not. So maybe this is what I need for closure. To get back out there. To make it a game. To make it fun. To even the score."

"Right. I get that. And I'm not saying it's a bad idea. It sounds completely, totally one hundred and ten million percent fun. But in the way that a reality show is fun. Then you're left at the end of the day with reality."

"And reality is I'm the loser, and they're the winners, and the only way I can see getting any sense of closure is to try to turn things around. Crying hasn't helped me feel better. Getting angry has helped me feel better. Hell, even shopping hasn't helped me feel better, and up until Todd left me I was just about sure there was no ill shopping couldn't cure. But here I am. Poke me in the heart like he did –" I say and demonstrate by poking myself in the chest – "And I turn into waterworks at a restaurant and camp out in the bathroom for an hour to hide. I hid in a frigging bathroom today. That's what I've been reduced to. I *have* to do something different to move on."

She nods, and even if she might not agree with me, she's my friend and she'll be there. "All right, crazy lady. You know I'm by your side, no matter what." She drapes an arm around me. "If this is what you need, then let's make it happen."

* * *

My crew is at the kitchen table. The reluctant Hayden, tall and leggy, chestnut brown wavy hair, librarian glasses on her face, sits next to me. Erin is to my left, her big red plastic hoop earrings waggling back and forth as she bounces a bit in her chair, brimming with energy as always. Her earrings frame her small, pert face, matched with her short, sandy brown, spiky pixie do. My sister Julia, with her reddish-brown-almost-auburn hair, long and lush, sits next to her. Hayden's married, Erin lives with her boyfriend, and Julia and I are the fully single ones.

My straight hair falls into my face, as it often does, so I push it behind my ears. I take a deep breath, then begin. "So here's why I called you all here tonight. To let you know Todd now drinks coffee in the morning, dines at the Best Doughnut Shop in the City, and gave up hard-boiled eggs. And, oh, there's one more thing. He and Amber had a baby and they named her Charlotte."

"Are you serious? They took your name?" Julia asks, her jaw dropping. "My God, sweetie, when did this happen?"

I don't want to relive this story over and over, don't want to feel that knife again expertly slicing me into pieces. So I recount the events of the morning as clinically as I can, then move on to the topic of the Meter Man before my throat hitches. There will be no more crying. Only marching forward, and this pursuit is my new battle cry.

"And now, my friends, we have Exhibit A." I grab my pirate girl purse and fish out the parking ticket from the inside pocket. I place the ticket on the table and smooth out any leftover wrinkles. "A solicitation for a date."

Erin claps. "Yay! I have been counting the days on my calendar until McKenna was finally ready to start dating again. This makes me happier than when my favorite men's swimsuit model books me for a massage." Erin is a licensed massage therapist and works at a day spa in Noe Valley.

"And we all know how happy that makes you," Julia says.

"What? He's hot, and I don't do anything but rub him down," Erin says, then takes another drink of the spiked hot chocolate that Julia, with her bartending skills, has so diligently provided for the crew.

"You know it's impossible to use the words *rub* and *down* in the same sentence without it sounding naughty," Julia says.

"I know," Erin admits with a grin. Then she raises her mug. "Let's toast to dating again. And maybe to a good banging."

Erin's a little, how shall we say, sex-obsessed? Not that there's anything wrong with that. But it's just the way she is.

"May the next man in McKenna's life be one of those heroes in a romance novel – rich, good-looking and perfect in every way," Hayden adds.

Julia pipes up. "Call me crazy, but I'm going to toast to you falling in love."

A part of me wants to raise a glass right along with her. To say wistfully, "wouldn't that be something?" Because, really, that would be everything I've ever wanted. It would be everything I *still* want. I was born a romantic, and bred a romantic, and I'm still one, even though I've been on a most decided detour for the last twelve months. Then I remind myself to stay focused on the prize because love smacked me hard on the cheek, leaving a red mark that still stings. I can't go looking for it again. If love comes along for the ride, so be it. But that feels a bit like winning the lottery right now, so I pull out a sheet of paper printed from a Web page. "This a background check on one Dave Dybdahl, the requester of said date. I ordered a criminal check. He comes up clean."

I hand the paper to Erin so she can pass it around for inspection. Then I reach for a printed photo I found on his Facebook page. "This is a photo of Mr. Dybdahl, otherwise known as Meter Man. But hold on, my little chickadees," I say, raising a hand for dramatic effect. I am going to be tough tonight. This is my moment, my moving on. "You see, my friends, this isn't just about one date, one guy, one parking ticket ask-out. Mr. Dybdahl is my first candidate for my new project. Project Boy Toy. Operation Kept Man."

A smirk forms on Erin's face. I have a feeling she will be my Number One cheerleader.

"Or even, dare I say it, dare I name it," I say, giving a little Rhett Butler twist to my wording, "Shall we call it the quest for the Trophy Husband?"

Erin cheers. "I love it."

I speak louder this time, as if I were delivering an impassioned speech, a call to action. "As long as men have traded women in for younger models, trophy wives have multiplied, grown their numbers. But what about the women left behind? The first wives, or almost first wives in my case? Do we scoop up younger guys? No. We don't. We cuddle up with the dog, we get to know the Chardonnay, we watch too much bad reality TV, and that is not ever going to help us move on. So I say it's time to turn this around and show that two can play at this game."

"Hear, hear," Julia says.

"But there aren't many Trophy Husbands out there. So just what does one look for in a Trophy Husband? What does one require?"

Erin raises a hand. "This is a relatively new breed of man, right?"

"Indeed, indeed he is," I say, nodding.

"And has this breed ever been spotted before?"

I shake my head. "Not in captivity at least. Not that we know of."

"So this is uncharted territory if you will."

I nod knowingly. "Very uncharted territory, my friends. Very virginal fields here. In fact, the Trophy Husband is so rare that few know what he looks like, what he eats, where one lives. Worse, we're not sure what he wears or what he requires. But we are going to find out. Because tonight marks the beginning of Project Trophy Husband."

Erin is eager to play. "We know one thing about a Trophy Husband. He has to be younger. A lot younger."

"You're right. But how much younger?"

Erin raises her hand, an excited student eager to keep answering. "Well, you're only twenty-seven, so there's not much wiggle room. So I say he must be between twenty-one and twenty-three. Super young, and super hot, and besides I can vouch for the appeal of a twenty-two-year-old male."

Hayden leans forward placing her chin in her long hands. Everything about Hayden is long. Her nickname is Giraffe. Her legs are endless and skinny. She has the flattest belly this side of Hollywood and equally thin arms. "Tell us more about this vouching."

I flash her a smile. I'm glad that she's going along with this. That I convinced her this project will be for the best. That it will be exactly what I need for the closure she wants me to have. I need Hayden's support in my life.

Erin leans in conspiratorially. "Well, you know I have a twenty-two-year-old client. Not the swimsuit model. But this other guy is a cyclist. He's on the LemonHead team or something. He comes in once a week, usually Monday mornings. I think that's his off day. He has a perfect body. Not an ounce of fat on him."

Julia points frenetically to the notepad. "Write that down. That's good. Perfect body. Not an ounce of fat."

"So basically we've got three things," I say. "Twenty-one to twenty-three. He needs to be hot. And he needs to be in spectacular shape. Where do we start? I mean, we have Dybdahl. Who's next?" Then I gulp. Because here's the part where I have no clue. Yes, I can tell you whether that skirt goes with that shirt, I can sing Karaoke in front of a crowded room, and I can make a prank phone call if properly dared. But ask me to find a man? I met Todd when I was twenty-one. I have been with one man for the last six years, and before then I was with boys. And not very many.

My momentary tough façade fades away, my all-business persona slipping off to the hall closet. I'm just McKenna right now. McKenna who got fooled by her boyfriend, who got duped and dumped and left, with a dress to send to consignment, dishes to be returned, and a cake that was donated to a homeless shelter. I hear the residents that day enjoyed it, and for some reason, that made me cry even more. Not that crying is hard for me. I'm the girl who listens to Billie Holiday and Elvis, and dreams of these foolish things. Things like love, and trust, and hope. Things like faith in another person. My heart winces for a moment, and a rebel tear forms.

Then, a voice pipes in, a small but strong little voice, coming from the other side of the kitchen. "What about the Fedex Guy?"

Hayden whips her head around. "Lena! What are you doing up?"

Lena smiles innocently. "Well, you always say he is cute and I heard you ladies say you were looking for a cute guy…"

Hayden scuttles her back to bed, this time shutting the door all the way and returning to the table.

"So tell us about your Fedex guy," Erin says with a sly grin.

But I don't return the grin. Instead, I feel a thousand seeds of doubt planting in my belly right now. I drop my head in my hands and mumble, "Who am I kidding? I'm not going to get a man. I don't have a clue. I'm the girl who was left at the altar. Who would want me?"

"Who wouldn't want you?" Erin counters.

"And besides, I'm twenty-seven. Shouldn't I be, I don't know, forty or something before I think about a Trophy Husband?"

"Why should age be a barrier? A Trophy Husband is just that – a catch. A pretty young thing. That's what we're going to get you, and you have what it takes to land a trophy husband whether you're twenty-seven or thirty-seven. You don't have to be Hugh Hefner's age, McKenna."

"Thank god for that, but I haven't dated, haven't been involved, and haven't a clue about men in the modern age. Hayden's daughter is trying to set me up with the Fedex guy! Because that's like the only chance I have and I'll probably bungle that one somehow." I look up at the crew. Their sympathetic eyes stare right back at me. "This is silly. I can't do this. I'm not cut out for this."

Erin slaps her palm on the table. "You are one hundred percent cut out for this. Men do this all the time and there's no reason a woman can't. They are always scoring younger chicks. Constantly. Besides, you have everything you need to snag a Trophy Husband. You sold your business for a ton of cash, you're loaded at twenty-seven, so why the hell not?"

"But," I say, starting to protest more, to tell them all I really want is a date with one good guy.

"No buts," Erin says firmly. "You have been in a funk for a year. Totally understandable, and no one expected otherwise. But this is your chance, McKenna. This is your light at the end the tunnel. Your way out of the sadness." Erin sounds so earnest as she reaches across the table and clutches my hand. "This is the perfect way to get back in the dating saddle again. By making it fun. By turning the tables. By having a crazy good time with a hot young guy."

"I know guys, but still. I just want –"

Hayden chimes in. "What do you want, McKenna?"

"I want," I start to say, and there it goes again. The hitch in my throat. The stinging in my eyes. The start of that horrible shaking feeling in my chest that says another round of tears are going to take over. I am so tired of this. I am so exhausted from the way my stupid emotions have controlled me. I don't want to be this person anymore. "I want to move on."

"Then do it," Erin says and bangs a fist on the table. This is a way to move on that's fun. You are single and you are hot and you deserve to have a grand old time on the dating circuit."

I scoff. "I am not hot."

"Have you looked at yourself in the mirror lately?" Hayden asks. "You're a babe, McKenna. You're tall and you're thin and you have good boobs."

Erin jumps in. "And you have that blond hair and your crazy, wild greenish-blue eyes."

"My hair isn't even natural! Guys, stop it, please!" I insist, covering my face with my hands, embarrassed by their compliments.

I hear heels clacking across the floor. Then I feel a hand on my shoulder.

"You are McKenna Bell." It's Julia. She's one year younger and has always been my biggest champion. "You are going to do this. Not only is this exactly how you're going to get over that d-bag, but this is bigger than you. This is bigger than all of us. You are Title IXing when it comes to the sport of dating. Remember in high school? You were the one who lobbied the school district for girls to play baseball, not just softball. And you didn't even play softball. You've never even played sports. You're the ultimate girlie-girl. But you did it because you have always been the biggest champion of Title IX."

In twelfth grade I petitioned the high school to let girls play baseball. I wanted to show that girls could handle the hardball, they could take the heat. It took nine months of campaigning, researching, petitioning and being the squeaky wheel. The school decided girls could play baseball in June of my senior year. Sure, I never caught a screaming fast baseball in a well-worn catcher's mitt, and probably never could. But that didn't matter. The girls who came after me did, and girls at Sherman Oaks High School still play baseball today. I know because I'm one of the biggest donors to the girls baseball program at my alma mater. They've won three championships in the last ten years. They rock.

"This is no different," Julia continues. "This Trophy Husband quest. It's about leveling the playing field when it comes to the sport of dating younger and hotter. This is your turn at the plate, and you're damn well going to take it."

"I am?"

"You are."

"You're sure?"

"I am so sure I'm beyond sure."

I take a deep breath and nod. I can do this. I'll treat it like a sport, a game, a project because those are things I can handle. Dating for a cause is far more manageable than dating for me. There's no safety net there. Here, I have a built-in shield. Maybe dating for sport is precisely how I should get back in the game.

The game of love.

"So no more guys your age. No more older guys," Julia says.

"Yes, ma'am."

"Todd was too old for you anyway. He was, what, five years older?"

"Six," I mutter. Todd's thirty-three.

"And guys older than you are now officially verboten. Got that?"

I nod dutifully at my sister.

"Raise your right hand," Julia instructs.

I do as told.

"Repeat after me. I solemnly swear, under penalty of breaking the girlfriend code that I will not date a man older than me."

I repeat her words.

"Because you are the poster child for this movement, and you are getting back on the goddamn dating wagon and finding

41

yourself a much younger, much hotter, much more fun man. Like Dave Dybdahl. Because Dave Dybdahl wants you, Dave Dybdahl asked you out, Dave Dybdahl wants you to call him right now."

Julia whips out her cell phone from her back pocket and plunks it onto the table. "I have speaker phone and I'm not afraid to use it. So get out your little camera because I know this is going to be a blog entry tomorrow on how to dress for a date with a hot young thing."

Hayden flashes me a contrite look when Julia mentions the camera, but I give her a reassuring wave, as I stand up and run next door to grab my computer and shoot on the iCam. Then in true junior high sleepover style – we might as well be in our jammies giggling and munching on popcorn all night long – I call Dave Dybdahl and ask him out, the computer cam capturing only my end of the call since he's still the innocent.

And the innocent says yes.

Chapter Three

"Have you played the newest Halo?"

Before I can even turn around to see where the voice comes from, I laugh.

"Have I played the newest Halo?" I repeat as I consider the video game shelves at the electronics store on Lombard Street where I've been contemplating buying Modern Warfare, which is next to Halo. "Am I breathing? Am I a sentient human being? I played it *and* saved the world from destruction in twenty-five hours, thank you very much."

Then I turn to my questioner and Holy Mary Mother of Hotness.

I drop the Modern Warfare box along with the camera box, and my jaw might have fallen to the floor too. I contemplate reaching down to the floor to pick it up so I don't die from the embarrassment of checking him out. Because my questioner is tall, trim, with light brown hair, kind of surfer boy length, and these crazy green eyes, the sort of green that's like the color of the sea, if the sea were green, only really it's blue. But you get the idea. His eyes are like Hawaii. He's wearing cargo shorts, flip flops, and a black Nor-Cal tee-shirt that shows off the right amount of tanned, toned arms. He's so cool and casual, and it's completely my favorite look for a guy.

He hands me the boxes I just dropped. "Here you go," he says, and I wish his fingers had just brushed mine. I'd take any sort of contact from him, even the barest trace of an accidental one.

"Thank you."

He smiles back at me immediately and then makes a little bow. "Twenty-five hours. Wow."

I'm a tad competitive so I can't not ask how he did. Plus, I'm totally digging his nearness to me right now. He's too hot to let walk away. Translation: he's blazingly beautiful and I want to keep looking at him. "Okay, I'll take the bait. What about you? How many hours?"

He waves a hand in the air.

"Oh c'mon," I persist. "I told you."

"Fine," he says, then lowers his voice to a whisper. "Seven hours."

My eyes go wide. "Get out of here," I say, and give him a quick push on the shoulder, like a teenage girl would do. Oh, those are nice sturdy shoulders. Too bad I'm not smooth enough to let my hand linger on his shoulders, or drop down to his chest. Right, yeah, because that would work — feeling him up in the middle of the electronics store. But still, it's a nice image to tuck away in the mental files.

He just shrugs casually.

I shake my head. "No, that's not how it works," I say playfully, enjoying the exchange with the perfectly handsome stranger behind the warm green eyes. "You can't just drop a little nugget like that and not give me the goods. Tell me how you got past the Forerunner Mission, because I was stuck there for hours, getting killed over and over."

I listen intently as Video Game Guy begins detailing his tactics, talking with his hands, moving his body back and forth a bit to simulate Master Chief's movements, the main character in Halo.

He has a nice body. Wait, he has a fantastic body. He has the kind of body that women driving cars slow down for. He has the kind of physique that turns a gal into a gawker. The way his tee-shirt falls just so tells me all I need to know about the flatness that lies beneath.

Then I remind myself to pay attention and focus, because it's rude to just stare at his belly instead of his face, especially when his face is so very lovely too. So I nod as he shares his gaming secrets.

I wasn't always into video games. In fact, it's not really accurate to say I'm "into" video games, per se. I'm not a gamer geek, though I did have a fondness for retro games growing up, since my parents used to take Julia and me bowling on Saturday and the Silverspinner Lanes boasted all the original arcade games like Qbert, Frogger, and, of course, both Pac-Mans. It's just that, well, I developed a particular predilection for shooter games after Todd left. I know – probably just a completely random little coincidence. And, to be fair, the video game habit didn't kick in the second he dropped his Vegas voicemail bombshell.

The first few months, all I did was cry at night in Ms. Pac-Man's fur, asking myself what I could have done differently, what had gone wrong, how I'd let him slip away. Was I not adventurous enough? Interesting enough? Pretty enough? Young enough? But it wasn't until I showed up for a Fashion Hound shoot in jeans and a wife beater tee, that I knew something needed to change. My videographer, Andy, took one look at me, and said, "We need a change, and we need a change fast. I have never seen you in monochromatic clothes before and your nails aren't even polished. You're a damn fashion blogger."

Then he told me when his last boyfriend had dumped him for another guy that he turned to Halo rather than self-loathing, and that made all the difference in the world. "Look, it's not like you and I are going to go out and shoot things for release, and that's why these games are perfect. It's like punching a pillow. Same idea – gets your anger out – but a hell of a lot more satisfying."

With my cheeks dry, all the tears sucked out of me, Andy took me to the electronics store and I bought my new therapy. A gaming console. At the end of each day, after I'd shot my videos, dutifully answered every email, and sketched out ideas for the next show, that little cluster of anger I'd been harboring was banging around, begging to be let out. So I'd turn that sucker on by ten most nights, and spend the next hour pumping bullets into bad guys. I was trigger happy, delighted to dispense ammo into whatever creatures came my way, gleefully, indiscriminately letting bullets fly, talking back to the screen: "Take that, you cheating scum."

I don't think I was talking to the game.

"What other games do you like?" the cute guy asks, and something about the question startles me. Maybe because it's so normal, and he seems legitimately curious. Then, there's the simple fact that we're having a conversation in the middle of an electronics store.

"Scrabble, Trivial Pursuit, Monopoly," I say with a completely straight face since I know he wasn't referring to board games.

But he picks up the baton easily, raising an eyebrow as he asks, "Clue?"

"Of course. And it was always Mr. Plum in the library with the candlestick."

"Interesting. Because Miss Scarlet was pretty wicked with that rope in the ballroom, if memory serves. What about Chutes and Ladders?"

"Let's not forget CandyLand either."

"What was your favorite candy destination in that game?"

"The vintage game, right? Not that new King Candy imitator?"

"As if I'd even be talking about that game," he says playfully.

46

I'm about to answer, when he puts his hands together as if he's praying and says in a whisper, "Please say Ice Cream Floats. Please say Ice Cream Floats."

I laugh, the kind of laugh I haven't felt in a while, the kind that radiates through my whole body and turns into a huge grin. "Of course. I wanted to live at Ice Cream Floats."

"I was all set to build a chocolate and licorice home in Ice Cream Floats. And this reminds me that I need to stock up on the classic games too. But I don't think they sell them here."

"I came here to stock up on a new camera." I pat the camera box. Then I dive into my best infomercial voice. "Did you know that when a cat pees on your camera it can't be resurrected?"

He shrugs his shoulders confidently, quirks up his lips. "Actually, I could fix your camera."

I give him a quizzical look.

"I can fix pretty much anything."

"Wow. That's impressive."

"Want me to try?"

"You really want to?"

"I do. Yeah," he says, as if he's digging the prospect of repairing the damaged device. "I really enjoy that kind of challenge. It's kind of like a game to me."

"The Fix-It game."

"Exactly."

"If you really want to, I'm not going to say no. I have it with me – it doesn't smell anymore, I cleaned it – because I wanted to make sure to get the same model." I reach into my purse and hand him the plastic bag with Chaucer's victim in it.

"I can have it back to you in a day or two."

"Great," I say, and smile, as I stand here looking at his fabulous face.

"But I would need your info to get it back to you."

Correction: As I stand here stupidly looking at his fabulous face. "Duh. Of course."

I give him my first name and number and he programs it into his phone.

"It was fun talking to you, McKenna," he says, then extends a hand. "I'm Chris McCormick."

We make contact, and I'm not going to lie – there's something about the feel of his strong hand in mine that just seems…right. Maybe it's the firm grip, or his soft skin, or the way his eyes light up as he smiles while shaking my hand. I don't want to let go. I want to go all black-and-white movie and have a simmering moment where his eyes smolder and, like magnets, we can't resist. He pulls me in, dips me, and plants a devastating kiss on my lips.

The kind of kiss that can ruin a girl for any other kisses for the rest of her life.

Chris McCormick is gorgeous, in a pure California sort of way, like sunshine and blue skies, like the ocean and its tides, but he's too confident, too steady to be young enough for my project. I bet he's, gasp, close to my age. I need to stay focused on my mission

"And if you want any more Halo tips, you can find a ton on Craigslist," he says.

"Craigslist!" I practically jump up and down in excitement, reminded of my overarching mission to find a Trophy Husband. "That's it. Craigslist! Thank you so much. I gotta go."

I head to the front of the store, plunk down cash for my camera, take a quick peek back at the Halo expert as I do, because it's a crying shame with that face, those eyes, that hair. Then I scurry back home.

Once at home, I open my laptop, and hop on over to Craigslist. Why hadn't I thought of this sooner? You can find anything there – new job, new couch, new BOYFRIEND. And I have Hayden's evil cat Chaucer to thank. If that dastardly feline hadn't peed on my camera then I wouldn't have wound up in the electronics store and I wouldn't have run into Chris McCormick, the Video Game Guy, with emerald eyes and a stunning smile, and I wouldn't have gotten the great idea to check out Craigslist, thanks to him. This is brilliant. This is epic. Finding a man-boy will be a piece of cake on Craigslist.

So I type the URL in and click on "Bay Area," while my blonde half-horse, half-dog, trundles on over and parks herself at my feet with a heavy sigh. She's probably counting down the hours until it's time for a swim in the San Francisco Bay, her internal doggy clock permanently calibrated to the rhythms of our day. I scratch her ears, then pet her head.

I start the Craiglist search with the Personals section and type "trophy husband" into the search bar. Hmm. Only one post with "trophy husband" in the whole Bay Area?

"I am 50 years old and am a successful stock trader. I am looking for a younger guy to share my good fortune with. Send a picture for mine. Be between 18 and 30 years old. I often travel to Europe, Asia, and Moscow on business and would love to bring you along. Must not have hang ups about being showered with gifts and being a trophy husband. I am a bottom as well."

This is it? The lone ad for "Trophy Husband?"

I soldier on and try "boy toy" this time, and it returns several options. I tap open the first entry because it boasts a promising subject line: *"Young guy looking for assertive older womam."*

So the young guy didn't exactly spell woman correctly. But let's hear him out.

"Extreme satisfacktion for the rite woman. Hansome male seek to belong to the woman who need to have nothing but the finest at her cummand. If your fantasy is to be in the company of a

beeuutiful, intelligent and discrete, sexy man than you is getting warmer."

Our public education system is much worse than I thought. After all, is it really that much to ask for one's potential next mate to be able to make a noun and verb agree? The answer, evidently, is yes. I try the next entry.

"Let me be your boy toy. I will obey your every order and serve your every wish."

At least *his* grammar is correct. And his writing has a nice rhythm to it, so I click through to his photo.

Ouch.

I am just going to pretend I didn't see that.

I squeeze my eyes shut. I remind myself that I am not a prude. I am not a priss. I am not weirded out by sex, or sexy people, or public displays of affection. But I am pretty sure – and I wouldn't have known this before because I have never seen one – that I am not into penis piercings.

So I move on to the next entry, trying my best to un-see what I just saw.

"I have a job, my own place in the city and am clean and well-kept," the next one writes.

What, like a lawn?

I hit the home button on the browser, returning to the safe haven of Google, then lay my cheek on the edge of my desk, wondering yet again if I am out of my mind. Because clearly I am not cut out for a Craigslist match. As much as I'd love to end my streak, I also wouldn't mind a bit more than a fling. I'm almost embarrassed to admit this because I'm supposed to be an independent woman – hear me roar – but I would really like to have a boyfriend.

The word sounds so high school, but I don't care. I don't want to be alone any longer. I want to be in love and carefree and have someone to talk to, laugh with, make fun of other crazy people in San Francisco with. Someone who would never even think of leaving me with two mixers and a vintage white dress.

I can picture it perfectly – a night out on the town, then we'd come home, turn on some torch music, he'd take me in his arms for a slow dance. Touch my hair in a way that sends sparks through me. Then a hand on the back of my neck, bringing me closer, lips meshing with mine. He'd slide his hand down to the small of my back, while laying a smoldering path of kisses down to the hollow of my throat.

We'd slow dance and sway, the kind of dance that's not for anyone else to see. The kind that's a delicious tease of foreplay, where every subtle move, every brush of the fingers, and dusting of the lips on shoulders, is the promise of what's to come. That dress straps will be pushed down, that zippers will come undone. Clothes will fall in the floor in a heap, tugged off quickly, as the dance moves to the couch and shifts into something horizontal. Slow and tender and tantalizing, each move, each touch turning me higher, sending me further into a dizzying state of longing.

My breath catches at the thought. Not only the prospect of kisses that ignite goosebumps all over me, but the possibility of someone who wants only me. Who only has eyes for me. Who wants to look at me, longing and lust in his perfect green eyes, and then throw me down on my couch, strip me naked, and bury his face between my legs.

Okay, so evidently, I both want a boyfriend and the kind of oral plundering that makes you quiver, and roll your eyes in the back of your head, and grab the guy's soft, shaggy hair, and shout his name over and over into oblivion.

Then curl up in his arms, safe and warm, and know he'll be there the next day and the next and even then some

Is that so much to ask for?

Love, and a talented mouth?

I close out of Craigslist. I'm not going to find what I really want there anyway.

Chapter Four

I model for the camera a cute little '50s style bateau neck blouse. Then, I step out of the shot, swap that shirt out for a form-fitting black V-neck with one purple shoe design emblazoned on the front. I step back in front of the camera that Andy holds as he shoots today's episode in my living room.

"What's it going to be, my fellow fashion hounds?" I point to the camera – the viewers. "You get to vote on how I'm going to dress for my first ever date with a Trophy Husband candidate. And be sure to watch the outtakes from my very first phone call to a potential candidate."

I pause for a second or two because this is the spot where Andy will edit in a few choice clips from my iCam-captured conversation with the Meter Boy. The clips include my awkward ask-out: "So should we meet in the Golden Gate Park near Shakespeare Gardens on Saturday?"

Am I the world's biggest dork or what? I couldn't have just asked Meter Man out for a cup of coffee or a glass of wine, or even, God forbid, something as simple as lunch. Nope, I had to go nuts and ask him to meet in the frigging park. He'll probably bring champagne and strawberries too.

Anyway, after my three-count pause, I give my traditional sign off, with a tip of the hat to my dog, who sits dutifully by my side. "That's all for today, you fellow fashion hounds."

Andy turns off the camera and I ask my usual question. "How was it?"

He gives me a thumbs up, his standard cameraman-slash-videographer response.

"That's why I like working with you. For the wordless thumbs up," I tease as I wind the cord to the microphone around my fingers, barely paying attention, doing the routine by memory. Then I hand Andy the microphone and wipe one hand against the other. Done.

"I'll have that online in thirty minutes," he says as he breaks down his gear, carefully folding up the tripod and shutting off his camera. His curly brown hair is a little shaggy as it hangs close to his brown eyes. Andy clucks his tongue a few times but says nothing. Uh oh. That's what he does when something's bugging him.

"What is it, Andy? What's bothering you?"

"I dunno," Andy says with a shrug, his hair flopping down in his eyes as he leans in to put his camera into its sturdy Port-a-Brace bag. "I guess I just don't think this is such a good idea." He zips his camera bag, averting my gaze.

"The bateau top? You really hate it that much?"

"You know what I mean."

"What do you mean?"

"You looking for this, this..." His voice trails off. He can't say the words.

"Oh c'mon. You probably want a Trophy Husband as much as I do."

"Ha. But not funny."

"Fine. Sorry. But I'm twenty-seven, you're twenty-nine. Don't you like a hot young guy?"

"Who I like is not what I'm worried about."

"Andy, what are you worried about?"

"Anyway." He hoists the bag on his shoulder and heads to the stairs.

"Hey." I follow him. "This is not how we have conversations. This is not how we talk. Don't walk away. Talk to me."

"McKenna." He sighs.

"What, Andy? What is it?"

"I don't think you should look for a guy on TV."

"One, I am not looking for a boyfriend. I'm looking for a husband," I say, correcting his word choice. But, to be honest, the two words are kind of interchangeable for me: A Trophy Husband feels a hell of a lot more like a boyfriend right now, especially since husband is a term I'm not terribly fond of, given how the almost husband I had dumped me. But Trophy Boyfriend just doesn't have the same ring to it. "Two, it's not TV. It's the Web. Three, it's not even about the guy. It's about making a point."

"Look, I'm just worried. You don't know what sort of problems this is going to create. I gotta go."

Then he shuts the front door behind him.

Later, after the video posts, Erin calls from work. "You are so totally wearing that bateau top. It's you. No question about it."

"Really?"

"Yes. I loved it and Julia loved it. I couldn't reach Hayden because she was meeting with a client, but I say two out of three ain't bad."

I laugh as I step away from the computer. "You're crazy. I can't believe you called the Brain Trust to survey them on my wardrobe choices."

"We're your inner circle. We are part of this project. We watched the video together. Well, on the phone, but together. And if viewers get to have a say, we get to have a say as well in every single aspect of the Trophy Husband quest, including how you dress."

"So it is written, so it shall be."

"And details, McKenna. We all wants details on the date."

As I say goodbye to Erin, I keep thinking how my girlfriends are always the ones who know what's best for me.

* * *

I told you so.

When I see those four words in my text messages, I tense. Was Andy right? Are there some weird problems already?

Then I see the name. Chris. The Video Game Guy with the green eyes and the smile that both melted me and made me want to climb up on his body and wrap myself around him.

I tap the message, opening it fully. There's a close-up picture of my camera, zoomed in on the the green on-button. He pulled it off.

I write back. *Wow, you are Mr. Fix-It.*

Minutes later he replies: *I'm having tee-shirts made up with that saying. In any case, your camera works again, so let me know how to return it to you.*

I stare at the message. For a minute. Then another. I don't know what to say. Should I say "by mail" is fine? Or "Should we meet for coffee?" But that would be so weird. He didn't ask to meet for coffee, just to give me back my camera. Am I supposed to suggest a meeting place? A means to return it? Carrier pigeon? Dog sled? I am entirely baffled, and so I stand at my kitchen table, the phone in my hand.

There's a scratching sound. I turn. Ms. Pac-Man is looking out the bay window at a squirrel racing across a tree branch. Then another buzz. It's the phone. Chris is calling. His name on the screen startles me, and I've lost all capacity to react normally. So for some inexplicable reason, I toss the phone onto the couch like it's a hot potato.

Crap.

That's not what I wanted to do.

It keeps ringing and I dive for it, hurtling over the back of the couch, landing on the cushions, and saving it from the disastrous fate of me having inadvertently thrown it away when a cute guy called.

"Hello?"

"Hey. So your camera is good as new, and I can get it back to you anytime."

"Great."

What do I say next?

"So, I go surfing every morning, but could meet up with you after that."

"Ocean Beach?"

"Yep."

"I actually have to go over in that direction tomorrow morning," I say, thinking that Shakespeare Gardens isn't far from the beach. "I could meet up with you tomorrow. What time?"

"How's eleven?"

"Perfect."

We pick a location and say goodbye. I make a note on my to-do list to buy some fresh tuna for Chaucer as a thanks for peeing on my camera. Then I remember I need to make sure Chris isn't an axe murderer who lures women with the whole "I can fix the camera your friend's cat peed on" line, so I Google him.

No wonder he knew so much about Halo.

He's not just some hard-core gamer. He's an expert, and he's a star in his field.

I find articles about him, links to him, stories in gamer magazines. I click on his Web site and see the video for his show, *Let the Wookie Win.* It runs online, and also on a cable network for gamers. Damn, the guy with the beautiful eyes, and the hair I wanted to run my fingers through, and who kissed me in my imagination that day, has his own TV show.

Impressed, I hit the play button and watch the most recent episode. Chris shares some inside tips on new games, from car games, to sports games, to shooter games. I watch as he demos a baseball game where you have to use your whole body and he simulates swinging a baseball bat. He looks like a star athlete, like a pro in the batter's box. He's ultra casual in a green Volcom tee-shirt, cargo shorts and flip-flops, demonstrating how to hit a hanging curveball. As he stands there in the batter box in his studio with feet apart and arms raised slightly, poised to hit, I can't help but notice again that, even with his shirt on, his midsection looks fairly trim. I could eat every meal off of abs like that.

Maybe he can be my video game tutor. Maybe we can play video games together, and laugh, and work on destroying bad guys as a team. And before we moved onto to the next level of the game, he'd turn off the Xbox, toss the remote onto the ground and slide me underneath him on my couch, one quick hand moving down to my hipbone, touching me there in a way that sends fireworks to every point in my body, before he smothers me in a kiss.

It's a kiss that doesn't leave any questions. It's a kiss that turns the rest of the world black and white, and only this, only him, is in color. A gentle slide of his tongue, an insistent press of his soft lips, and I am his, swimming in the sweet heat. I can feel the kiss in the center of my being, and then it radiates all the way to my fingers and toes. I want to be kissed like this always. By someone who knows how to kiss me, and who says in how his lips consume me, in how his hands hold on tight, in how he shifts his hard body against mine, that he wants all I have to give.

I've become hypnotized as I watch him, mesmerized by the way his body moves with a fluid sort of grace. I place my palm on my chest, imagining my hand is his hand, that he's touching me gently for the first time, that he's exploring my body, eager to learn how I respond to his touch, to his strong hand on my breast, then my belly, then my hips. I'm him for a moment, fingers trailing across my mid-section, ready to sneak under the fabric of shirt, spread his hand across my stomach and…

What the hell? I'm in some sort of trance, touching myself, pretending he's touching me.

I put on the brakes. If I let this go further I'll be a tongue-tripped mess when I see him tomorrow morning. And we just can't have that, can we?

* * *

My timing is impeccable.

I do not want to miss a chance to see Chris walk across the sand, so there's no reason for me to be on time when I can be early.

I park on Taraval Street along Ocean Beach, get out of my car, and wait. I try my best to look busy, fiddling with my phone, and checking compartments in my purse, but when Chris appears on the horizon, surfboard in hand, wet suit tucked under his arm, I freeze.

And then I blush, remembering what he did to me in my mere imagination yesterday. I'm sure he'll be able to tell, to read it in my eyes. I really should pretend I'm not watching him. But it's impossible not to. I didn't look away during that scene in Casino Royale either when Daniel Craig emerged from the water. He wears board shorts, low on his hips, and a pair of flip flops. I watch him as he walks through the sand, closer, closer and there, now I can say without a shadow of a doubt that I would like to lick all those water droplets off his chest and his abs and then run a hand down his body to sear into my memory the feel of that kind of firm outline.

He's lickable. He's kissable. He's chat-up-able. He's precisely the type of guy a girl can fall into some kind of crazy crush for. He catches my gaze, and I should be embarrassed, I should act as if I'm not staring, but there's this fluttery feeling inside me, and I want to hold onto it, especially because he's looking at me and not letting go either. Those green eyes of his are the definition of dreamy, and if I were a writer, I'd find a way to pen a song about them, how they draw me in, romance me, entice me.

Soon, he's mere feet from me, scratched-up surfboard by his side, in all his glistening, ocean-ed up glory. Neither one of us says anything for a few seconds, and it's the kind of silence that's filled with unsaid things.

With wishes, with hopes.

Mine at least.

"Hey."

"Hi."

"Thanks for meeting me here," he says, as a wet shock of hair falls across his forehead. He pushes it back.

"Thanks for being a surfer," I say, then I want to kick myself for sounding so goggly-eyed.

He flashes me a grin and walks to his car, a sporty red car that I recognize as being one of the newest hybrids. He stows the wetsuit in the trunk, then slides the board into the rack on the roof, stretching his arms to lock the board in place. I picture myself slinking into the narrow space between Chris and the car, the look of surprise on his face, then wicked delight, as he closes the gap between our bodies. He's warm and wet from surfing and sun, and I'm warm and wet from him, and I imagine him lazily tracing a finger down my arm, enjoying the way the slightest touch sets me ablaze. I'd shift closer, my hips inviting him to become a puzzle piece that locks into place with me.

I force myself to shutter those images, because they have no bearing to reality.

He opens the passenger door, reaches inside and hands me a bag with the camera in it.

"Good as new," he says.

"How did you fix it?"

"I can't give away all my secrets now, can I?"

I smile. "I suppose not."

"But maybe you'd be willing to tell me your last name now that I've fixed your camera."

Another smile. Another nervous laugh. "McKenna. McKenna Bell."

"Well, thank you for letting me fix your camera, McKenna Bell."

"Maybe if I'm lucky, the cat will pee on my router next."

He smiles, then runs a hand through his wet hair. There's something so effortless about the way he moves, so natural, that I don't even think he's aware of the effect he has on women.

Of the effect he has on me. I want to run my hands down his chiseled chest, exploring the lines between his muscles, the way his stomach is outlined so firmly. I want to know what those arms feel like wrapped around me, pulling me in close. I want his hands on my hips as he teases me and taunts me with sweet kisses on my cheeks, my eyelids, my forehead. Then his tongue flicks across my earlobe, and I gasp with pleasure. He pulls back, a satisfied little grin on his face before he returns to my neck, burning up my skin in an instant with those lips that were made to mark my body.

Then I stop the fantasy from going any further. If I don't, I'll just start panting right here on the sidewalk, and he'll know I was this close to undressing myself for him.

"I should go, Chris. But thanks again. This is awesome."

There. I've got plenty of self-control, and he surely can't read my mind and know I was about to become liquid heat for him.

"Yeah, watch out for cats," he says, and that's all. That's it. No flirty comeback that says his imagination is running wild too.

Then it hits me. A guy like this – successful, hot, and totally talented – must have a girlfriend. He must have many girlfriends. He has that California ease about him, a laid-back charm that reels girls in.

As I walk away, he calls out casually, "Or maybe the cat will pee on your iPod." I look back, meeting his gaze even from several feet away as he adds, "If I'm lucky."

I drive to Golden Gate Park with those three words playing on repeat. *If I'm lucky. If I'm lucky. If I'm lucky.*

Then I tell myself he's just a flirt. Because there's no other reasonable explanation.

Chapter Five

All I can say is Andy was wrong.

Because there is nothing pathetic about Meter Man.

Nothing at all. At least from a distance. He is walking toward me right now and I like the way he walks, I like the way he moves.

I'm camped out on a bench in front of Shakespeare Garden, surrounded by the ponds and hills and bike paths of Golden Gate Park. Though Shakespeare Garden has a big name, it's a little spot, maybe the size of a large backyard or a private courtyard. Twin columns frame wrought-iron double gates, a brick walkway cuts across the garden, and a sundial stands in the middle.

I like this spot for many reasons, but especially because Todd and I never went to Shakespeare Garden in all our time together. It's untouched by the enemy.

I met Todd because we took the same bus to work every morning, him to his PR shop and me to the fashion brand, Violet Summers, I worked at before I started my blog. Almost every morning I watched Todd get on the bus, slightly disheveled, wearing a blue, white, or blue-and-white striped button-down Oxford cloth shirt and khaki pants. He always sat in the same spot, two seats from the front of the bus. I started inching closer, a seat a day. Two weeks later, I was in the seat behind him.

"Nice day, isn't it?" I said.

"Yeah, and that's quite a feat in this town." He turned around, his elbow resting on the back of the seat. "You know what Mark Twain said about San Francisco?"

His eyes lit up, he was excited, like he was about to share the coolest, most unusual quote in all of literature with me. But like everyone else who's ever set foot in San Francisco, I knew it by heart, so I said loudly, "The coldest winter I ever spent was summer in San Francisco."

He smiled back, his light blue eyes twinkling mischievously. He didn't say anything for a few seconds and his sneaky silence unnerved me. Then he said, "Not that one. This one." Then he quoted the Mark Twain saying that no one ever quotes about San Francisco, but one that is more beautiful, more original, more sexy. "It is the land where the fabled Aladdin's Lamp lies buried – and she, San Francisco, is the new Aladdin who shall seize it from its obscurity and summon the genie and command him to crown her with power and greatness and bring to her feet the hoarded treasures of the earth."

I felt warm all over, lured into his gaze, his charm. He wasn't like every other straight guy in San Francisco who rattled off the Mark Twain summer-winter line as if he were the cleverest male in all the universe. Todd was clever, he was charming, he was smart. He knew something other people didn't know.

Sweetly, he added, "I like that one better."

We chatted until my stop. As I stood up I reeled off the one San Francisco quote I knew. "You know what Oscar Wilde said? *Anyone who disappears is said to be seen in San Francisco.*"

"Don't disappear. Have dinner with me this weekend."

"I won't. And I will." Then I hopped off the bus and counted down the hours until the weekend.

I cringe now at the memory, but that was all it took back then. I have always fallen first for cleverness, for smarts, for wit. Looks have been secondary.

That's about to change, I tell myself, because looks are clearly where Dave Dybdahl excels. He is ridiculously handsome. He's wearing jeans, work boots and a white ribbed tee-shirt. Twin straps from a purple Jansport backpack line his shoulders. Even from a distance, even from twenty feet away, I can tell – heck, anyone within eye-goggling distance can tell – he is fantastically cut. His shirt isn't snugly, but it's near enough to his body so I can make out the firmness of his pecs underneath the fabric, the absence of any fat on his belly, the slight bulge of his biceps peeking out right where the shirt sleeves end.

His body isn't the only thing chiseled. As he nears me, I take in his well-designed face again, like a model, an escort, with Johnny Depp-esque cheekbones, deep blue eyes and a subtle wave in his brown hair. I take my headphones out of my ears and gently lay my iPod on the bench. I smile, a little nervously, and stand up. I am not sure what the proper protocol is – shake hands or hug? I rack my brains trying to remember how a first date usually starts. It's been eons, entire evolutionary stages it seems, since I last went on a date. I could say the wrong thing, do the wrong thing, mess up the secret handshake that experienced daters know, a sure cue I'm a newbie. I'm probably on some Do Not Date list, like that Do Not Call List.

I err on the side of friendliness, reaching out for a quick, short hug, his hands touching my hair briefly.

"Hey there to you," Dave says.

"Good to see you again."

I sit down on the bench. He follows suit. I reach for my iPod, tucking it safely away in the small lime green vinyl purse I switched to for the date. The purse is covered in yellow lettering listing "hello" and "goodbye" in a smattering of foreign languages. It's my date purse. This purse hasn't gotten any action in years.

"Were you just bopping out on your iPod?" Dave asks.

Bopping out?

But at least we have the iPod icebreaker to get the conversation going. "Billie Holiday. I love the classics. I'm kind of a retro girl." I gesture to my shirt.

He nods a couple times. A thoughtful look descends on his face, like he's considering what I just said. "I gotta admit, I'm pretty good with music. But you stumped me right there. I don't know him. What does Billy boy sing?"

"No, no. Billie's a girl. Billie's a lady actually. You know Lady Day, first lady of jazz?" I say to prompt him, trying to jog his memory. I've got to believe the gears in his brain simply sputtered for a moment, hit a tiny roadblock. He'll get back on track, I tell myself. So I keep going. "You know she sang *You Go To My Head, Embraceable You, These Foolish Things*?"

He shakes his head a few times and lets out a deep breath. "Damn. You just really got me there. Who does she sound like? Katy Perry? Rihanna? Beyonce?"

"Love those ladies, but yeah, I'm gonna have to say none of them."

So what if we don't have the same taste in tunes? It's not the end of the world. Focus instead on his firm, sculpted body. "So, did you have to work today?" I ask. Meters, after all, can be violated on weekends too.

"No, but I did take a training class this morning."

I brighten. I love to learn new stuff. "What did you learn?"

"It was fascinating." He leans forward on the bench, closer to me. His eyes really are magnetic. They're like the color of a clear blue sky, a sapphire even. "You see, there are sections of the city that are moving to resident-only parking during certain times of the day, but at other times of the day, other people, not just the residents, can park there too. But on weekends, you see, it's only the residents. But during the day, like, anyone can park there. So it's just really, you know, it's just you need to focus on when the cars are illegally parked and when they're not." He furrows his brow.

I nod a few times, waiting for him to explain the part of this that seems so complicated to him. Dave closes his eyes for a second, squeezing them shut, repeating a mantra, "Residents only – only residents can park. Other times – anyone can park." He opens his eyes and breathes out. "Yep. Yep. Sometimes I need these little sayings to help me remember."

"Like a mnemonic device."

He purses his brow. "Like pressurized air and stuff?"

I shake my head. "No, that's pneumatics," I say, pausing for a moment to tuck my hair behind my ears. "You know, it's like a memory aid?"

"A memory aid!" He's excited, delighted at the idea. "That's great. That is exactly what I need."

"Well, that's what a mnemonic device is. It's like ROYGBIV to help you remember the colors of the rainbow."

"This is so great!" He slaps his thigh in excitement. "Where do I get one of those?"

I breathe in, trying to center myself. Focus on his eyes. Focus on his biceps, his belly, his pecs. Focus on anything other than what's coming out of his mouth. A good body can cover up a lot of flaws. A centerfold physique can mask a poor intellect, I try to tell myself.

"Yeah, you don't buy them. It's just something you use, a saying, for instance, to help you remember."

"Cool beans."

"So, Dave, what's next after being a parking meter attendant?"

His eyes light up. "You know, I think I'd really like to be a parking consultant."

"Really?" I'm going to need to just zero in on his eyes and hair right now. Wait, I have a better idea. I'm going to think about him without a shirt because that may be the only way I will make it through this date. "What does a parking consultant do exactly?" I ask, resting my arm on the back of the bench and pretending Dave is taking off his shirt. That's right, one sleeve off, then the other, then the shirt goes over your head.

"You know, I'm like not entirely sure, but I just gotta think there's a need for someone, like a real expert to consult on parking matters."

Just toss that shirt on the ground right now. "Oh sure, parking matters. That's gotta be huge."

His eyes light up. "You think so?"

"Definitely," I fib. Just undo that belt buckle next and maybe the button on your jeans too. "Huge demand for parking consultants."

"Yeah, so maybe, I could get an office and start a web site."

"Absolutely," I say enthusiastically. Now just stand up and unzip those jeans and loosen them. Yep, drop them on the ground. "And advertise your services too," I add, keeping him going.

He snaps his fingers and tosses his head back, amazed at my seeming brilliance. "Like on billboards around town. That is such a great idea!"

Oh it is, indeed, so just stand there now for a minute in your snug black boxer briefs and let me gaze.

"Hey, what are the colors of the rainbow? That ROYGBIV thing?"

The words that come out of his mouth are a gigantic buzzkill. So I put his clothes back on. The jeans come up, now they're zipping, the button is going back in its button hole, the shirt comes back down over his oh-so-wonderfully sculpted abs – I feel a momentary pang as I say goodbye to them – and then I mentally tuck his shirt back in.

He's not Chris. He's not even close. I can't even undress this guy in my imagination. Call me crazy, but I want the complete package. Brains, humor, looks, hands and tongue and lips that turn me inside out, and most of all, a kind heart.

"Red, orange, yellow, green, blue, indigo, violet."

* * *

"How can I put this tactfully? He wasn't exactly playing with a full deck, know what I mean?" I state as I take another drink of my *Purple Snow Globe*, a new drink Julia is testing out on me at her home away from home, Cubic Z in the SOMA neighborhood where she tends bar. It's got raspberry juice, gin and sugar crystals on the rim.

"Like missing a card or two, or maybe an entire suit?"

"Jules, he could have had an eight-incher and I wouldn't have cared."

Julia raises an eyebrow. "Have you ever had an eight-incher?"

I shake my head. "Not that I know of."

"Let me tell you something, sister. It's not like you need to break out the ruler to know when it's eight inches. You just know."

I place the martini glass down on the counter and look straight at her. "You've had eight inches?"

"Why do you think I dated Donovan three times? It wasn't his conversational skills," she says, then tells me she'll be right back. A customer at the other end needs a refill.

Julia is, quite simply, a heartbreaker. First, she's sexy and curvy and has that kind of reddish-auburn hair that drives men wild. Second, she's a bartender. Men dig that. They think a chick who can mix drinks is manna from heaven and Julia is. That's why Donovan kept returning to her. She kept going back to him because

69

he was, evidently, endowed with a Magic 8. But she wanted other attributes kicking on all cylinders too.

"All I am saying is," Julia begins after she's returned to my corner of the bar, "Looks and, well, you know, size, aren't all that. You've got to be able to have a conversation with a guy. When I find someone I can actually talk to that's when I'll know I've found the one."

I flash back to Chris, to our easy conversations in the store, and earlier today by the beach. Fine, we only chatted for a few minutes each time, but there was something sort of instant in our connection. The kind of quick banter and repartee that makes a girl think of possibilities, of days and nights, and music and laughter. That makes a girl think songs were written for them. As I take another swig of her concoction, I let myself linger on those words again. *If I'm lucky.*

Did he mean those words? Was that some subtle way of saying he wants to see me again?

I click on the browser on my phone and go to his Web site. The connection in this bar is molasses slow, so the page won't fully load, but his picture appears.

I can't help myself. I smile. My stomach executes a teeny-tiny flip. I trace a line across his face. He's so handsome, with that sun-kissed hair, and his bright green eyes. He has this fabulous smile, like he's a happy guy, like life is good, and he'd bring nothing but pleasure and wit and great conversation into my life. I should call him. I should email him. I should ask him out on a date. We could be so good together, we could sail off into the moonlight.

And there I go, in my imagination. Time slows, and the bar disappears, and it's just Chris and me. He's taken me out for coffee, or dinner, or a movie. Or better yet – a round of Candyland at the kitchen table. We could even invent our own rules that involve kissing every time you have to go back a few spaces.

Or more.

Kissing that leads to so much more. I close my eyes, and picture a kiss that starts sweet and soft and slow. Then, his hands cup my face as if he's claiming me, saying *you're mine* with his lips and his hands and the way he draws me in close, his thumb tracing a line along my jaw. It's such a small gesture, but such a poetically possessive one and I arch my back, inviting more. In one swift move, he pulls my chair to him, sliding me between the V of his legs. His fingers thread their way into my hair, and I lean into his hands, reveling in the way they feel against the back of my head, as if he's holding me in the exact way he wants me, in the exact way I want to be held. My breaths grow louder as he kisses me hard, craving the taste of my lips crushed against his. A groan escapes him, telling me he doesn't want to stop; he only wants more of me.

He breaks the kiss, stands, and reaches for my hips, quickly pulling me up. I sway, still lightheaded and probably will be days. But he steadies me with one hand on my waist, and he looks at me with such dark desire in his eyes, with a fierce kind of hunger as if he has to have me, touch me, be with me.

One look like that and I am his for the asking. For the taking. My heart pounds harder and my pulse speeds.

It's clear we're not playing Candyland anymore. We're going off the board, he's shoving the game and all the pieces to the floor in one strong sweep of his arm. The cards and the markers scatter, clinking on my floor, and I don't care about anything else except the the way he lifts me up on the table, and moves his hand from my throat to my chest to my waist, as if he knows instinctually how much I love having my hips touched, like he knows all the spots on my body that can drive me wild without me even having to tell him. He can find them in the dark, without a map. He needs no direction. The playbook to my body is in him, his head, his heart, his hands. He knows what I want. He knows how I like it. He wants to give it to me. Soon, I'm breathless, and we're chest to chest, hips to hips, and I'm grasping at him, my hands sliding around to his perfect ass, so round and firm, and I grab hold of him, desperately needing the friction of his body against mine, even though we're fully clothed. His hands explore me, feathering against the exposed skin of my thighs, then sliding inside the hem of my skirt. Teasing, tempting, inching higher, and if he keeps going like this I am going to lean my head back and gasp in pleasure. Something I'm dangerously near to doing as his fingers reach the deliciously agonizing point where I want him most. Discovering how ready I am for him. Wickedly delighting in knowing I am full of a crazy kind of longing for him, that my body calls out for his. Oh, I could so cry out his name right now, let him have me, take me, taste me. Let the world know he drives me wild.

Then I stop the fantasy from going any further. A guy like that – funny, charming, into video games – would never be into a gal like me.

Besides, there is no moonlight.

Chapter Six

I stare at my computer screen, as if the solution to finding a guy who'll fill my heart with gladness and take away all my sadness lies somewhere in the machine. Because Meter Boy was a bust, and Craigslist is not my cup of tea, and I don't know where to go next. It's not as if I'm terribly good at the bar pick-up scene. Does that even work anymore? I haven't a clue about how to date, let alone how to run a dating contest. Why did I ever think I could pull this off? I'm a fashion blogger. I know which shirts go with skirts, and where to find the screaming deals. I don't know about men anymore.

The doorbell rings. I straighten up and head over to the front door, quickly checking my reflection in the nearby mirror. All clear. I peer through the peephole.

The Fedex Guy is back.

He really is cute. He has blond hair and brown eyes, a combo I love. I'm reminded of Lena's suggestion that I consider him as a candidate. Maybe the eight-year-old was right.

"Hold on, I'll be right there," I shout, then I peek at the mirror, fluff my hair, bite my lips for color, and smooth my tee-shirt, a pale yellow number that I picked up at a little shop in Petaluma that's my best source for quirky cool tee-shirts. This shirt has an illustration of a mechanical horse and the words "Saddle Up and

Ride" on the front. I've worn it a few times on my show, and viewers love it, and so does the store that sells it since I've sent a ton of business its way. I also worn it once when I picked up Hayden's daughter from school to help her out. I got a few cold looks from the other moms that day. Whatever. It's not like it says "Saddle up and Ride Me."

I open the door and do my best to assume a sexy smile, but not quite a come-hither one. It's a delicate balancing act. And I am so out of practice at the art of seduction, I'm beyond out of practice. But I give it my best shot. *Be sexy, be bold.*

"Hello," I say slowly, drawing out each syllable.

"Hi there. Got a package for you. Want to sign?"

"I would love to sign your package," I purr back.

He raises an eyebrow, and all my self-confidence depletes to zero. A withered balloon.

"Just tell me where." I return to my professional voice. No wonder I haven't landed a date. I'm abysmal.

He points to the clipboard he's holding, tapping his pen against the spot where he wants my name in ink. I sign as directed, then look straight at him, not up or down, so he must be right about 5'10" too. I try again, going for simple and direct this time. "McKenna Bell, there you go. And what's your name?"

He hands me the envelope and smiles back. "Steely Dan Duran."

I crack up right there on my doorstep. "What's your name for real?"

"It really is Steely Dan Duran. My mom was a huge Duran Duran fan."

"Evidently."

"And my dad liked Steely Dan. So they compromised."

"That is the very definition of compromise."

He nods and gives me another smile, and that's exactly why I like it when he brings me packages. That sexy sweet grin is precisely why he's the type of deliveryman a girl can fantasize over. So I lay the envelope on the table by the door and decide to see if he qualifies. Because maybe this is my parking karma at play – Triple D might not have worked out, but perhaps the universe is delivering the best man to my porch in the form of Steely Dan Duran.

"So is your mom like a child of the eighties or something?"

"Apparently. I think they were listening to Duran Duran and Steely Dan when I was born."

Oh, he practically walked right into that.

"And that would be in 1982?" I ask with a wink.

He laughs. "Ha. '90."

Twenty-three. Perfecto. "So Steely Dan Duran. Would you like to go out some time?"

He takes a step back, as if I've just asked him to drink hemlock.

"Scratch that," I quickly add, crimson racing to my cheeks. Why did I ever think I could pull this off? "I'll just take that back."

But Steely Dan Duran will have none of it. He steps towards me and places a hand on my arm. "I would love to take you out to dinner."

"You would?"

He nods vigorously. "I was just surprised that's all. But please don't take it back because I would love to go out. And I would love to be the one to do the asking. Would you like to go out with me?"

"Yes."

I'm ready to dance a little jig, kick my heels up in the air a la Gene Kelly. Maybe it's *not* that hard to find a Trophy Husband after all. I make plans with Steely Dan Duran for next weekend and head back inside. I reach for the envelope he dropped off and rip it open.

And there goes my happy mood.

My jaw drops as I read a letter from Todd's attorney, requesting joint custody of the dog. Now that he has a house in Marin, and a baby, and a yard, he's claiming the dog is better suited with him. I can't believe he has the audacity to ask for this, but then he's the same person who didn't leave my favorite restaurant when he ran into me even though that would have been the courteous thing to do.

I read more, pushing my hands through my hair, hard against my scalp. My brain is about to officially pop when the papers request three canine sleepovers each week, and then I nearly gag when I see Amber's name as well on the claim – Todd and Amber Frank.

I pick up my phone and call him at work. He answers immediately and I don't bother with niceties. I launch right into it. "You have got to be kidding me. The dog is mine, and you haven't so much as taken her for a walk in the last year, let alone a sleepover."

"And that needs to change," he says.

My mother lioness instincts kick in. I'm the one who trained the dog, walked the dog, fed the dog, took her to every vet appointment, threw tennis balls to her in the water. He didn't want the dog when he left me for Amber. He doesn't get the dog now. "The dog stays with me."

"I figured you would feel that way, and that's why I hired the best attorney, so perhaps you should take it up with him. I believe you have his number on the legal papers."

Then he hangs up on me.

I slam the papers down on the credenza and huff back into the kitchen, practically ripping the fridge door open. I need a Diet

Coke and I need one now. I grab one from the lower drawer and angrily pop it open, taking a thirsty first gulp.

I savor it because I find few things in life as singularly satisfying as the sound and feel of a can opening. The Diet Coke trickery should have been my tip-off that things with Todd wouldn't work out. I'd be working or paying bills at the kitchen table and ask him to please bring me a Diet Coke. He knew about my first sip fixation, he knew I derived uncommon pleasure from the very first bubbly sensation, from the taste of the virgin cold metal on my lips. Yet, he would always ruin it for me by opening the drink himself and taking a sip while he mosey-ed on over to the table to deposit the can in front of me with a devilish little smirk. He'd give me this look, this "Aren't I cute for taking the first sip when I know you love it" look. And he'd think it was endearing. I tried to explain every time that I was serious about this. I really wanted my own first taste.

I know it's not a big deal. I know that disagreeing about the first sip of a soda isn't the reason he left.

I can enjoy every single ounce of this soda all by myself right now. I can enjoy the money from the sale of The Fashion Hound. I can enjoy the silence in this house.

But I can't always. Because tears now roll down my face as I look at this legal letter, this cold, business-like language that we have been reduced to. We used to spend nights tangled up in sheets, and lazy afternoons only with each other. We used to be each other's rocks and each other's lovers, a potent combination of reliance and passion that would see us through all our days.

Then there was one night in Vegas, and everything shattered. Right down to the dog. We adopted Ms. Pac-Man three years ago from the San Francisco Humane Society, picking her out at that same jinx-you-owe-me-a-coke moment when she tilted her blond head to the side and won us over with those big brown canine eyes. We were a threesome, a little family unit.

Now, she's some pawn to him.

My chest heaves, and I bring my hand to my mouth, shaking with sadness. Embarrassed that this is who I am now.

Alone with a soda and a letter from a lawyer.

I try so hard to be tough, to be impervious to the whole fucking world.

But moments like this?

I miss, and I miss, and I miss.

I miss being cared for. I miss being loved. I miss being considered. I wipe a hand across my cheek, my mascara streaking. I used to love him so goddamn much. I didn't stop loving him the second he took up with Amber. And now he's with her, really with her, and I'm here in my kitchen, with only the first sip for comfort as he tries to take my dog from me.

As if she's some sort of toy for his new wife, his new kid, his new life without me. Ms. Pac-Man hears me and ambles on over to sit at my feet, looking at me as if to ask if everything's okay. I tell her yes, even though it's not true.

I sniffle, reach for my iPod, and pick *Sailboat in the Moonlight* by Billie Holiday. I might as well just stick my finger in a flame, but I can't resist the way she sings about tender lips, about dreams coming true, about all the things I ever wanted.

I may be hunting for a boy toy, but somewhere inside of me I am still longing for someone to sail away in the moonlight with.

Only, I no longer have that luxury. I can no longer ask for or expect those things. So I take a breath, I dry my tears, and I crush the empty can of soda in my hand.

Crushing my dreams of a love I can't dare to hope for.

* * *

Steely Dan Duran isn't much better. For starters, we're dining at Baby Doe's all the way in Marin County on the other side of the bridge. I don't go to Marin often. There's not much need because the city has everything I want. But let me tell you all you need to know about Baby Doe's.

Baby Doe's is where you took your prom date in 1977. It hasn't changed a lick since then. It's the same dimly-lit restaurant, with the same red pleather, same puckered booths, same orange chandeliers, and probably serving the same steak and baked potatoes and garden salad.

Steely Dan Duran loves this place. Had I known he was taking me here, I would have found a gentle way to nix it. I would have perhaps delicately suggested something more interesting, like sushi, Japanese, Thai. Heck, a pizza joint or even a taqueria somewhere on Fillmore would be better. But Steely Dan Duran wanted to surprise me. So he picked me up, wearing dark brown slacks, a striped shirt, and a tie of all things, and kept the location a secret as we drove down the 101 in his sky-blue Buick. When we arrived, he came around and opened my car door – I will concede he gets points for that – and said "Ta Da!"

"Your baked potato, ma'am." The waiter lays the side dish on the table for me, complete with a sprig of parsley and a pat of butter. Then he presents a baked potato to Steely Dan and heads back to the kitchen to retrieve my date's steak and my chicken.

I gesture to the spud, my right index finger adorned with a flashy pink stylized ring in the shape of flower petals that complements my maroon lightweight sweater, one of those wrap-around numbers with a super slim tie around the waist and a low-cut neck. I'm wearing a white lacy cotton camisole underneath it and black capri jeans with ballet flats. I lean in and say playfully, "Maybe we could get bacon bits for the potato too."

Steely Dan stops his fork in mid-air. "Would you like me to ask for some?" He's so earnest, so thoughtful, but there goes another joke, falling to the floor with a dull thud. "I was just kidding. I don't like bacon bits."

He looks at me quizzically as if I have just told him I have three ears and one of them is on my forehead. "You don't? Why not?"

Um, because they're gross?

"Just not my thing," I say lightly. Then I happily spear a hearty glob of potato innards and smile broadly to show I am enjoying every second of our evening. Just as I am about to taste the spud, he reaches for my wrist and stops me.

"We have to say grace first," he says.

"Oh." I place my potato-filled fork down.

He lays his hands out on the table, gesturing for mine.

"Maybe I could say it," I say, sort of teasing him. Because I wouldn't know the first thing about saying grace. I'm all for religion, but have never been into it personally. My parents were completely non-religious. He shakes his head. "The man should lead."

"Excuse me?"

"The man should lead. That's why I was the one to make sure to ask you out. Because the man should be in charge. Guide all the decisions. For the woman. For the family."

"About everything? Like dinner? Like work? Like where to live?"

He nods. "All of that. And also, what a woman should wear. For instance, I would never let my wife leave the house until I had approved her outfit."

I crack up into peals of laughter. "You are a funny guy! That is the funniest thing I've ever heard."

His face is stony. "I wasn't joking."

Oh. That's not going to fly. I think I'm about to officially walk out on a date for the first time. Yep. I definitely am.

"Goodbye Steely Dan Duran. This girl dresses herself."

* * *

"So maybe I should call this off," I tell Hayden as I flop down on her couch after the cab drops me off, and she lets me into her house.

"Because of one bad date?"

"Two bad dates. Dybdahl was a total bust."

"Oh right. Good point," she says as she settles in next to me.

"And to top it off, Todd now wants custody of the dog."

"You're not going to let him, are you?"

"Of course not. But do I have a choice?"

"Well, I'm a patent attorney, not a pet attorney, but I'll look into it for you," she says. "Because that is a cause I can totally get behind. Project Dog Custody."

I pull myself into a sitting position on her couch. "And I thought you weren't fond of pets," I tease.

"Not the ones that pee on my furniture. But the good ones, like Ms. Pac-Man? Yeah, I'll help you win this battle, that's for sure."

I glance at the couch and the cushion I've been sitting on. "That's not your way of telling me Chaucer peed right here?"

"No," she says with a laugh.

"So, um, Hayden. Do you think I should just throw in the towel on the Trophy Husband thing?"

She gives me a rueful smile. "McKenna, I think you should do what makes you happy. Would it make you happy to throw in the towel?"

I shrug. I don't have an answer. I don't know what makes me happy except for the dog. "I think I'm going to go spend the rest of my night with my dog."

I head home and Ms. Pac-Man is so excited to see me that I give her a kiss on her wet snout. She licks my cheek, a big, sloppy dog kiss, and I love it. "There is no way I will let anyone take you away from me," I tell her, and I know she understands. I know she wants to be with me. She loves me unconditionally, and I love her the same.

I pat the side of my leg, her cue to trot along by my side as we head into my bedroom and over to the closet. "Let's look at clothes for tomorrow's shoot, shall we?" I say to my favorite creature.

She sits down and watches me as I survey my clothes, her eyes on me, her tail still wagging. I can't resist. I bend down to pet her once more. The dog is kind of my soulmate, and maybe I will keep fighting the good fight. For her. I won't let Todd win. Not when he's throwing punches so far below the belt.

Chapter Seven

"So that makes me O-for-2 in the old Trophy Husband date department, so you know what I did after being told I should have my clothing approved? Call me crazy. Call me wild." I lean into the camera and stage whisper. "I went online and bought myself some awesomely hot tops. Like this one!"

Then I let Andy pan over my shirt – a peach colored tee with ironed-on female superheroes like Wonder Woman and Bat Girl. It says *Ladies Night* on it. Then I share the shopping info with viewers. "Oh, and one last thing. I am totally striking out in the date department. I'm basically abysmal at dating. A total dating dork. So I might have to call this whole thing off, my fellow fashion hounds. Unless you can send some pretty young things my way, this girl is going to have to be over and out."

I place my palms together in a plaintive sort of plea, then we stop rolling, and I exhale. Being the Fashion Hound requires my utmost focus on appearing upbeat, confident, sassy and totally kickass tough. I am take-no-prisoners on camera. But off-camera, I can be more of myself.

Andy and I begin our usual wrap-up routine. "How was it?"

He gives a cursory thumbs up, and walks out to his car, parked in front of my house. I follow him. He hasn't gotten over his little snit fit from last week, evidently.

"Andy, can we get this sorted out please? I hate fighting with you. Can we go have a cup of coffee or something? Or come inside and have a Diet Coke?"

He doesn't answer. But he doesn't start the car either. Instead, he rests his hands on the steering wheel and stares off down the road, not looking at me. I seize the window of opportunity, the temporary break in the clouds. "You know, a Diet Coke? Were both junkies. It'll be fine."

He sighs heavily, then looks at me. "Maybe you shouldn't spend all your life trying to make a point. Anyway, I have to go."

But if I don't make a point, then where would I be? Back in the bathroom of the diner I can't go to anymore? Huddled in a stall, too scared, too embarrassed, too damn wrecked to leave?

I head inside and pull my phone from my back pocket. The message rush won't start for an hour, but the habit is hard to break. I walk upstairs, thumb tapping in my password. I click on the envelope icon and once I do, I simply stop walking, stop moving, stop doing anything. I rub my eyes, sure I am seeing things. My inbox is bursting with 307 new messages. I wonder if I have an email virus, something that sends spam with abandon to my email address. But as I scroll down and scan the messages, most of them have similar headings: Re: *Let the Wookie Win, Saw You on Wookie Win, From Let the Wookie Win.*

Then I notice a few other subject lines: *TH project, regarding trophy husband, I'm a candidate.* "I click on an envelope icon and read a random note. "Hey there. Def interested in your quest. You need better guys! I am your man. Would love to see you anytime."

I open the next one: "I could be your arm candy anytime."

Then the next: "I have been waiting my whole life to be kept."

Finally, I reach the top message in the queue. It reads: "Blame the Cat" in the subject line. I open it.

Hey there, McKenna. Has your neighbor's cat caused any more trouble? If he has, you know where to find me. Also, I checked out your blog and I love your current thread, so I talked it up in my own show, Let the Wookie Win. You might get a few emails. Watch today's episode and you'll see why...

I let out a happy squeal, even though I have no idea what the episode is about. Then I look around to make sure my neighbors didn't see or hear me. I return to the message, and I'm sure there's a smile plastered on my face simply from seeing his name.

I hit play and watch the episode as he demos a car racing game, then shares some viewer tips from Call of Duty, analyzing each one. Chris finishes the moves and then says to the camera, "All right, I've heard you clamoring for another segment of *Games People Play*. For those of you new to the show, this is where we step away from the console, from the computer, and we talk about, well, you can figure it out from the title. This one, guys, you're going to love. There's a hot chick out there in the video blogosphere who's looking for a man to keep. I know a lot of you are twenty-three or under and if you are, she wants to hear from you."

He rolls into a clip from *The Fashion Hound* from a week or two ago when I first introduced the quest. Then the video cuts back to Chris and he says, "Dudes, don't sit there and watch me any longer. Go pimp yourself to the cause, go get into the Trophy Husband sweepstakes. There's a babe out there willing to put you up and all you have to do is look good. Just think, you can probably play games all day long. So go play this game and tune in tomorrow for the next episode of *Let the Wookie Win*, the one gaming rule you should always follow. Later."

I don't move. I am frozen at my desk. *Hot chick.* He called me a hot chick. He called me a babe. There is hope for me after all. I write back: *A few emails, Chris? More like 300! I should take you out to lunch to say thanks.*

I hit send as the nerves of asking a guy out swoop down on me. It's just a business-y lunch, I tell myself. I totally didn't just ask him out on a date. I merely proposed a thank you meal with a fellow video fiend. He may not even write back today.

But Chris does not make a woman wait. Thirty seconds later a reply arrives.

I never turn down a free meal. Want to have lunch at Fritz' Gourmet Fries tomorrow?

More than anything in the world right now.

Chapter Eight

Hayden adjusts her glasses, a sign she's about to go into lawyer mode. "Now, bear in mind that my area of specialty is in patent law, not pet custody."

"First the disclaimer," I say. I'm hanging out at her house that night, stretched out on her couch with my laptop, her doing the same. Greg's at a business dinner, and Lena just went to bed.

"But I looked into Todd's claim, and even though it's ridiculous you can't just ignore it. If you do, that's when problems start to occur."

"Are you saying he can just come and take the dog?"

"No. I'm not saying that. And to be honest, possession is nine-tenths of the law, so you have that in your favor. But what you need to remember is San Francisco is a city that enacted an ordinance elevating pets above property in family law matters. Pet owners are now legally considered guardians rather than pet owners, so you have to take this seriously."

I roll my eyes. "Seriously?"

"It is a left-wing paradise, isn't it? So you need to start rounding up documents. To show you take care of the dog. Vet bills, Vet records."

"What about her health insurance? I pay for that too."

"I still can't believe you have pet insurance. But yes, gather all those documents. Along with pet food receipts, receipts for toys you bought for her."

Something about her list energizes me. It's fuel for my never-let-Todd-win mission. "I brush her teeth every day. I buy the dog toothpaste online, so I have all the records of the times I buy her toothpaste."

Hayden snaps her fingers and points at me. "I like. Yes. That. Do that. Anything. Amass it all. Because if it gets to a court, or a judge, or even a pet mediator, you want to show that you are this dog's sole owner."

I tilt my head and give her a chiding look. "Hayden. You mean *guardian*, don't you?"

She smiles. "Yes, counselor. I mean *guardian*."

"They really have pet mediators?"

"This is San Francisco. How many domestic partnerships and common law marriages do you think involve pets?"

"A lot."

"And this reminds me. When you do snag yourself that Trophy Husband, let's make sure the dog's *guardianship* is established from the get-go."

"Speaking of, I need to do some whittling."

"Want me to help you?"

"You would?"

"I told you I'm here for you. So if you're doing this, you better make room for me," she says, and scoots closer to check out the pictures together as I return to my inbox, which is bursting with more than five hundred potentials thanks to the power of Chris' show.

"How about this guy?"

"Ooh, I like that one," Hayden says, pointing to a dark-haired hottie with a seductive smile.

"Let's move him to the potential keeper folder," I say and slide his email over with a flourish. I wonder briefly if I should tell her about my kinda-sorta-maybe date with Chris tomorrow. I don't even know if he's twenty-three, though I doubt it. But as Hayden's eyes widen and she points merrily to a cute blonde guy, then vehemently nixes a so-so redhead, I decide I'm better off keeping Chris to myself for now. If my one reluctant friend is now fully backing the quest, I need to stick with the plan and adhere to the oath I took at her house a few weeks ago.

Besides, it's just lunch.

Lena pads down the hall, wearing her black and orange San Francisco Giants pajamas, and holding *Green Eggs and Ham*, still her favorite book. "Mom, I can't fall asleep. Can you read one more book to me?"

"I'll read to you," I offer. "These emails are making my eyes glaze over."

"Can I see?" Lena leans over the couch to see the pile of emails stacked up, virtually, in my inbox. "What are all those emails, McKenna?"

"She's just trying to sort through some boys for potential dates," her mom says, since Hayden tends to be pretty open with her kid. Ergo, so am I with Lena.

"Yeah, cause the Fedex guy was a dud," Lena says, repeating back what I told her a week ago when she asked.

"Total dud."

"So do you like any of these boys?"

"I'm not sure yet."

"Don't worry. You'll find a nice boy. I want you to be happy. My mom wants you to be happy. We both want you to find your sailboat in the moonlight."

I tear up again. My friend and her kid know my favorite songs. They know what my heart wants, even though my brain rarely listens to my heart.

* * *

"You can never go wrong with fries."

"Or with forty-seven varieties of dipping sauces for fries," I add as I survey the list of ketchup substitutes that Fritz's offers. Fritz Gourmet Fries is on one of my favorite streets in the city. Union Street happens to boast some of the best shopping in the city, with arty boutiques and funky little shops where I often find purchases to show my viewers. But honestly, the only reason I am thinking of my second favorite pasttime – shopping – is that if I don't I might be eaten alive by the butterflies in my belly.

Chris is so cute. So handsome. So delectable. And I am sure I am going to do something to mess up this sorta date because I haven't a clue how to date. I've been with one guy since I was twenty-one, and I don't even know if this is a date with Chris, but I want it to be one. Because he thinks I'm a hot chick, and I think he's a total babe, and I've already imagined the passion with which he kisses and the sparks his fingers send through me…

I focus on the menu because if I don't I will surely do something incredibly inept.

I scan the list of forty-seven dipping sauces – pesto mayo, spicy yogurt peanut, creamy wasabi tapenade, spicy lime, roasted red peppcr. They all sound delicious.

"If I told you my favorite French fry dip was ketchup would you think less of me?" Chris leans in as he asks the question, the menu spread out in front of him on the table, his light brown hair falling across his forehead. He's wearing jeans and a green tee-shirt with a picture of a cartoon squid on it. The squid's cool, but I mostly like the shirt because it shows off his arms, toned and strong. I'm wearing a flouncy skirt, a purple scoop neck top, a matching necklace with small purple plastic squares strung together, and my Mary Janes.

"Dude, you drove my views up by fifty-five percent in *one* day," I say, referring to the viewership stats from yesterday when he first mentioned me, because if I say what I want to say – *How could I think less of you, you beautiful man* – he'd run. "So as for how you like your French fries, well I say you could eat them in a boat, you could eat them in a box, you could eat them with a fox –" I cover my face with my hands. "I can't believe what I just said."

Chris laughs. "You're reciting *Green Eggs and Ham*!"

"I know." I look up, a little embarrassed. "Well, Chris. The cat's out of the bag. I'm kind of a dork."

"Nah, that's just a good book."

I shake my head. "I can't believe I said that, like it was a punchline or something. I think it was because I was reading it to my friend's kid last night. She's eight and she still loves it." Chris looks at me, listening, but I feel kind of silly again. Why does he bring out the awkward in me? Oh right. Because I want to run my hands through his hair, and I want to find a million reasons to touch him, his hands, his arm, his legs. Because, yeah, that's awkward.

Chris' green eyes sparkle. "But would you eat them in a house? Would you eat them with a mouse?"

"Not in a box, not with a fox, not in a house, not with a mouse," I fire back, and I could kiss him for the way he now makes me feel un-awkward.

"I would not eat them here or there. I would not eat them anywhere."

"Okay, Mr. McCormick. Pretty damn impressive."

A waiter pops by our table, fresh-faced and smiling, with a face so smooth he looks he hasn't even started shaving yet. "And what can I get you fine folks today?" he asks, rather jollily.

"I'm gonna go a little wild and order some French fries," I begin.

"Yeah, go nuts!" the waiter replies cheerily. "What kind of sauce would you like with that?"

"I'll tell you what. Why don't you surprise me? Just pick your three best, any three, and bring them back to me."

The waiter's eyes light up. He's thrilled to have been entrusted with such an important task. "It will be my pleasure."

"And I'll have the Mediterranean salad with that," I add.

"And for you?" The chipper boy asks my lunch companion. Chris orders a chicken sandwich, French fries, and extra ketchup. The waiter returns to the kitchen. I launch right back into conversation.

"So now I feel I must regain some street cred in your eyes, so I'll tell you that the last time I watched her kid, I read her the lyrics to one of my favorite songs to teach her new words."

"And what would those be?"

"Well, now she knows all about an airline ticket to romantic places and a tinkling piano in the next apartment since I read the lyrics to *These Foolish Things* to her," I say, then I want to clamp my hand on my mouth. Why don't I just tell him to whisk me away and bury me in kisses that make me forget where am I as the world disappears and time slows to one delicious moment with him? Because I don't think I gained any points by serving up that romantic mushfest to him.

"You should know that, one, you didn't lost any street cred by reciting *Green Eggs and Ham*, two, you definitely gained even more coolness for sharing one of my top five favorite songs of all time, a song I would only ever admit I liked to a girl," he says, and

I hide a grin because I didn't just mess up. "And three, I know the words to *Green Eggs and Ham* because it was my little sister Jill's favorite book, and I taught her to read way back when."

"What a good older brother."

"Thank you. I'm one of two brothers. Youngest boy, and Jill's the only girl."

"And is Jill out here in the Bay Area?"

He smiles and shakes his head. "Nope. She's in New York. Actress. She landed a part in this new Broadway musical called *Crash the Moon*. It opens soon and I'm going to go see her. I'm really proud of her."

"I've heard about that musical. It sounds amazing."

"Yeah, she's pretty stoked about it. We text and email a lot, and she's been telling me about it. But I think the director is also making her kind of crazy."

"I have to imagine directors of musicals probably have a way of doing that."

He smiles back and this time I notice his teeth. They are nice, straight and white.

"So I wanted to thank you again for mentioning my show on your show. That's what this crazy video world is built on, right? Cross promotion."

"Speaking of, that's something I wanted to talk to you about," Chris says.

My heart sinks. I had thought this was a date. But it turns out he may have a business agenda. Then I tell myself it's better this way. I wouldn't know how to date someone like him for real.

The waiter appears with our salads, sandwiches, fries and sauces. He deposits the plates on the table, hurries off, then returns with water. He clasps his hands together, almost like he's praying. "Now, can I get you anything else? Anything else at all?"

I shake my head and Chris says no. The waiter leaves.

"Is he like the happiest person you have ever met?" Chris asks.

"Yeah, I'll have what he's having."

"So, I have to tell you. I looked you up after I gave you back your camera," Chris says, and I find myself hopeful again because he looked me up. He dips a French fry into the ketchup. "When you finally gave me your last name and well –" He stops himself, shifts gears a bit, then resumes. "And then when I did and saw you were this big Web personality..."

I laugh once. "Hardly."

"Anyway, I added you to my RSS feed and started watching your show every day, even though, I have to say, I'm not into fashion. But I watched it because..." his voice trails off again, and I want to fill in the gaps. I want to script what's unsaid. *Because you thought I was cute too?* But I can't let myself hope. Hope leads to disappointment. "And then when you talked about the dates you went on and how they flopped, that's when it hit me. I could send you some of my viewers. Because they're young and hopefully somewhat cool."

"And I've gotten pictures from about five hundred of them!"

"And I'm sure some of them are dorks like most guys are, but you never know, right?"

"There were some good ones in the crop it seemed."

He pretends to blow on his fingernails, the sign for being too hot to handle. "Damn, maybe I am good at this matchmaking thing." Then he becomes serious and asks, "So I have to ask, is this for real?"

"For real?"

"Yeah, for real. I mean, it's funny. Don't get me wrong. I think it's a hilarious storyline. But it's a storyline, right? It's a game and all, but are you actually going to go through with this?"

"What do you mean, go through with it?" I ask, dodging the very thorny question of will I say "I do." Because for me, frankly, this isn't about the "I do" portion. It's about the trophy aspect. It's about the catch. And, I suppose, what landing such a prize might say about me. That I can move on. That I am over Todd. That he's not the only one who wins.

Chris takes a bite of his chicken sandwich, chews, then says again, "Yeah. Are you really looking for a Trophy Husband?"

I furrow my brow and pretend to be all thoughtful. "Hmmm…I've always thought a pool boy would be nice. Even a cabana boy."

He laughs. "So it's kind of a joke."

"No. My ex-fiancé left me at the altar last year for a college student he met and married in Vegas the night before our wedding. He's thirty-four and she's twenty-one now, and I think it's royally unfair that men can do that and women can't."

He puts the sandwich down and looks at me intensely. Seriously. "Your ex-fiancé is a complete asshole for a million reasons, but most of all because he'd have to be crazy to leave you."

"Thank you. Thank you for saying that."

"It's his loss, McKenna," Chris says in this kind of fierce tone that makes my stomach execute a few loop-de-loops. Is he flirting with me? How do I even flirt back?

I do what I do best and turn the questions back on him. "What about you? Maybe you should be a Trophy Husband."

He laughs.

I look at him pointedly, my eyes open wide. "Well, why not?"

"Well, um…" he stammers. He seems slightly uncomfortable. My cue to keep going.

I egg him on. "After all, you encouraged your viewers to throw their names in the hat. Maybe you should too. Maybe you could be a Trophy Husband, Chris."

He starts blushing, his cheeks turning a faint shade of red.

"You're blushing!"

"Yeah, well…"

"It's kind of cute actually."

"Thanks, that's what I was hoping for. Cute blushing."

"You don't like the sound of *cute blushing*?"

"It's not very manly, now is it?"

I soften a bit. "Why are you blushing?"

"I just don't think I'm Trophy Husband material," he says, kind of sweetly, a little innocently.

"Well, why not? Are you already a husband?"

"No, that's not it."

"So what then? You could be a prize catch, Chris," I say, and he smiles.

Actually, it's more like a grin.

"I appreciate that. I really do."

"Well?"

He sighs, then puts his hands on the table. "I don't think I meet the *other* qualifications."

"What do you mean?"

"I don't ever say my age on my show, but I'm twenty-nine," he whispers.

"Holy fuck! You're practically middle-aged."

He laughs. "Yeah, I'm an old man, McKenna. But keep that between us. I want the kids to think I'm cool. Besides, somehow, a viewer updated my Wikipedia page and it says I'm twenty-three, and I never got around to correcting it."

"Well, I am so glad we resolved this issue. You are clearly not in contention."

He reaches out and briefly touches my arm. Then he looks me straight in the eyes and says, "It's a shame."

He's serious. At least, I think he's serious. My breath catches, and my heart skips, and I want to go back in time and rewrite the age rules for my Trophy Husband game. Let them be thirty or younger, even though that makes no logical sense. But hearts aren't logical and my heart wants Chris to play. I don't know what to say next though, so I return to the one topic I can handle — business. Besides, I made a pact with my girlfriends. They've had my back, and I can't let them down. This isn't about me. This is about the point, the pursuit, the game.

"So, what can I do for you? You're helping me and I don't want this to be a one-way street. I've got to be able to do something to help you out, though truth be told, most of my viewers are young women and I'm not sure how many are gamers."

"You play," he points out. I like that he's willing to change directions so quickly, that he doesn't keep harping on some philosophical question, or practical question, neither of which I have answers to.

"Well, yes, but I'm just a casual fan."

"Exactly. And a lot of young women are. In fact, the female gamer is one of the fastest growing categories in the whole video game business," Chris says excitedly. "I'm actually starting a new show in a couple months targeted for women who are sort of the casual online gamers, but new to the console games. And I need to get the word out, promote my new show."

I nod. "So we do a cross-promo, maybe? You're thinking some of those girls who watch my show might want to try a little Guitar Hero?"

"Guitar Hero? Did you just say Guitar Hero? That game isn't even made anymore."

"Oh, I didn't realize that," I say, feeling stupid. "Someone gave it to me a few years ago. It looked kind of fun. I think I played it once, but I haven't been able to find my copy since."

"Hey. I didn't mean to sound like a gamer snob."

"It's okay. You didn't."

"I mean, it's a totally awesome game. You should definitely play it more. I was just saying I think chicks are getting into other games too. The shooter games, the sports games, even just trivia games. They're all taking off into the mainstream, especially with hot young chicks, like yourself."

It's my turn to blush now. He said it again. *Hot chick.*

"Oh look," he points at me. "Now you're cute blushing."

"I guess we're just a bunch of cute blushers."

He smiles again, and then places his palm on my wrist, and that single gesture of his hand on my skin melts me. And while there's a part of me that wants the kitchen table fantasy with Chris, I also want the other side with him too. The part where I let him into my heart and my soul, the part where we get to know each other. Because right now, I want to lean forward and taste his sweet lips. I want to hop into his lap and wrap my arms around his neck and smother him in kisses. I haven't felt this way in years. I don't even know what to do with all this wanting. I want to spend the day with him. To wander around the city, and stop in shops, and grab a coffee, and talk, and get to know him, and ignore my phone because he's so much more interesting than any text message could ever be. I look at his hand, resting on me, and it's almost enough for me to throw the whole Trophy Husband quest away, to just ask this guy to spend more time with me. But I don't know how to back down, or how to let go. Most of all, I don't know how to begin to let someone into my wounded heart. I don't even know if my heart is healed, or if the scar tissue has just grown so thick and knotty that no one can ever touch me again.

So I return to a subject I can handle. Games. "Speaking of games, I kicked ass at Qbert when I was a kid. My parents were totally into this retro bowling alley near our house, and it had all the classic arcade games."

"I was a Mario Brothers man myself."

I reach for a fry and dip it into a lime-ginger sauce. "I loved that game. I used to play for hours, bouncing from square to square, trying to avoid Coily and the gremlins, trying to jump on discs. I went from level to level, to the white and green level, then to the ones where you just saw the tops of the squares..." I take a bite of the French fry. "I miss Qbert. And I mean the real Qbert, with the diagonal joystick, the pixilated graphics, the funky sounds."

I notice Chris has a devilish little smile on his face, that one side of his mouth is curled up.

"What?"

"I have Qbert."

"For the Playstation, you mean?"

Chris shakes his head. "I have the real Qbert."

"The arcade Qbert?"

He nods proudly a few times.

"You have Qbert, arcade Qbert?"

"The real deal. In my living room."

"I am having visions of eighth grade now. I am having visions of Silverspinner Lanes and me getting the high score, punching my initials in for all the world to see."

"Bet you can't beat my high score."

"Oh, you think you can take me on in Qbert?"

"I do."

"You are on."

He holds out a hand to shake, and I have to wonder if he's trying to find ways to touch me too. If he's liking this little flirty stuff as much as I do. If he's imagined more than flirting, more than lunches, more than kissing too.

"You'll have to come over sometime and we'll have a Qbert match," he announces and then digs back into his chicken sandwich.

Now, take me to your house now. Show me Qbert, and let me play, and kiss my neck as I move the joystick. Then brush my hair aside and flick your tongue against my earlobe, and make me shiver so much that Qbert dies and I don't care, because all I want to do is turn around and have you kiss me so deeply and so much that I can feel your kiss all the way through my veins.

* * *

After we finish, we leave the restaurant. As we walk down Union Street, I notice that Chris is a few inches taller than I am. I don't often meet men who are much taller. I like the feeling of being next to someone who is.

"You know something about those fries?"

"What about those fries, Chris?"

"I will eat them in the rain. And in the dark. And on a train. And in a car. And in a tree."

"They are so good, so good, you see."

Chapter Nine

I close the blinds in my bedroom and slip into bed. I pull my computer onto my lap, settling under the covers. It's been ten hours since my lunch with Chris and I know one thing for certain: I want to see him again.

I knew pretty much the second I sat down with him, the instant we started talking, that I wanted to see him again. I think it works that way more often than not. The whole idea of liking someone. You just kind of know, right away, within minutes usually. There was a moment, maybe when he was talking about having looked me up online, when he paused and then moved on to something else. It was almost as if he was going to say that he thought I was cute, or something. Or maybe it was when he said *it's a shame*. It felt like something went unsaid, something *good* went unsaid there at our lunch.

Maybe I'm fooling myself. Maybe I'm just wishing and hoping for things I won't have. Things I don't even know how to deal with. Even if he does like me, what would I do with that? How would I fit that into my grand scheme?

I don't have the answers though, so I focus on the here and now. On the feeling. On the wish and the hope that I might see him again.

I open an email message to him and start it *in medias res*.

So that one time I played Guitar Hero I only made it through two songs. I think I have two left hands.

I hit send, then slide out of bed to brush my teeth. Once they are scrubbed and buffed and clean as can be, I turn off the light in the bathroom, then the bedroom, telling myself to close my computer for the night, to resist hitting "send and receive." But self-restraint has never been my strong suit. So I hit that tantalizing little button in my email program, just in case.

The icon whirs and a few seconds later, I'm rewarded.

That is so not OK on so many levels. I will teach you. Meet me at that electronics store on Thursday at 2 p.m. for a lesson.

I write back.

Lesson? You teach at the computer store?

His response comes moments later.

That's why I was there when I met you. I teach newbies how to play video games once a week. Like yourself, evidently. Go ahead and say it. I am a full-fledged Internet geek.

I reply.

You are indeed. But then again, so am I. I will see you there in two days.

Then I do shut my computer down for the night, as Ms. Pac-Man sleeps at the foot of the bed. My laptop occupies the left half of the bed, the side Todd used to sleep on. I sleep alone, haven't shared a bed for the last year. Except with a computer and a dog.

I snuggle under the covers and close my eyes, thinking about Chris and how he blushed something fierce when I asked him to be a Trophy Husband. Of course, I was just playing around.

Still, he would make a good candidate if he were twenty-three. Then I wonder what actually constitutes a good candidate.

I say the words quietly aloud.

"Trophy Husband."

I break it down.

"Trophy." Then, "Husband."

As I separate them, as I pull the adjective away from the noun, I find I don't really like them apart, I don't really like the second word by itself.

Husband. Husband. Husband.

For the first time since I started this project that word echoes in my brain. That title, that role. But I don't want to think about the practical application of the title. Because I'm not ready to think about what it means. That's why I have answered the question in other ways. That's why I have turned the question into one I want to answer, a question about politics, about equality between the sexes, about what women can do, about proving the naysayers wrong, about making a point. Or about my friends, and how they want me to do this to move on. How I need to need move.

Even though now I kind of want to move on to Chris. So I close my eyes, and think of him, and the way he blushed, and how he touched my hand, and how he said all those nice things that make me want to curl up with him instead of my Mac.

I've let my mind wander to him so often already. I've pictured snapshots in time with him – on my table, kissing him by his car, making out with him on my couch. But today, for the first time, I felt as if maybe, just maybe, he might want those things too.

And so, I let the images rush by. I picture him here with me, walking into my bedroom, seeing me here in my bed with just a tank top and bikini underwear on. He drinks me in, his eyes saying how much he wants me. He doesn't lower the light. He wants to see me, to watch me, to savor every inch of me. He walks over to the bed, crawls up onto it, and straddles me. He's pinning me, a knee on each side, then he brings my wrists up high above my head. I'm helpless, but I don't care. Because each move he makes stakes his claim to me. He buries his face in my neck, kissing me behind my ear, and making me groan. He runs his tongue down to my chest, cupping my breasts through my top. I'm completely aroused in an instant and I wriggle under him. He flashes me a quick and wicked smile, knowing he's having the desired effect already. But he doesn't give in to the arch of my hips just yet. Instead, he lets go of my wrists, removes my top, and kisses my breasts. First one, curving his hand all the way around and tugging at my nipple until I say his name in a hoarse kind of voice. Then the other, so deliciously, that all I want right now is to know exactly how his mouth feels against the center of me. I writhe underneath him, trying to guide him faster down my flesh to the throb between my legs. And soon, soon, he listens to my body, inching down my waist, kissing my belly button, and then nipping at my hipbone. I cry out.

"Please touch me," I say. And he knows what I mean and how much I need to feel his tongue swirling a delirious line across all that liquid heat in my core. In one swift move, my panties are off, and his face is between my legs, and my hands are in his hair, and I am mindless with pleasure as his tongue swirls against me. My knees fall open, blood rushing through my veins, heating my body, as I see him, feel him, picture him here with me. He is masterful, his tongue painting dizzying brushstrokes through all my wetness. I grab him, bring him closer, wrap my legs around his shoulders. He grips my calf, running his hand over my smooth skin as he buries his face between my legs, spread open for him and holding him tight at the same time. I rock into him, and I can't stop. I can't hold back. I don't want to. He goes deeper with his tongue, as if he can't hold back either, as if he can't resist drinking me in, as he grips my hips and devours me with his lips so intensely that the neighbors may soon know his name. Drenched with desire, I am panting and moaning, singing his name and wishing he were the one doing this to me right now.

Chapter Ten

I brush last night's solo ride from my mind when I see him. I have to. I can't let him see that he's already done so many things to me. That he's unraveled me and I've come for him. I have to back this all up and let him be my gaming tutor.

"So do you teach a lot of newbies how to play Guitar Hero?"

"Not as much as a few yeas ago," Chris says, then hands me a black plastic guitar. The guitar is a cross between a real guitar and the sort of miniature kid-size guitar someone might give away in a grab bag at a party for musically-inclined ten-year-olds.

"What can I say? I'm a retro-loving gal." I point to my flirty little vintage blue dress with a cherry pattern on it.

"That's a totally hot dress, and if you keep pointing to it, it'll make it hard for me to concentrate on giving you lessons."

I hide a wild grin at the compliment, as I drop the guitar strap over my head, slinging the plastic instrument across my belly. It's not mere fashion happenstance that I chose this dress. It accentuates all my best assets, and I also love it, so I feel good when I wear it. And with his comment, I'm left to wonder if he's entertained after-hours thoughts about me too. How far they went. If he touched himself, if he pictured me doing things to him, if I made him come too. My mind is awash in dirty thoughts that are dangerously close to making me too turned on to function. So I shove away all the delicious images of Chris undressed, naked, in his bed, lost in thoughts of me.

Chris turns on the Xbox and then hits the on-button on my guitar. We're in the former car stereo room at the electronics store, only now it's been converted into a sort of gaming living room. Customers can come here and test out all sorts of games on the various consoles. Or they can get lessons from the master once a week.

The game whirs on, a picture of a dark pink mountaintop, set against a black night sky, appears on the gigantic television screen hanging on the wall in front of us. Chris moves closer to me, taps a few buttons on my guitar to click past that screen, then the next, then the next. I want him to touch a few more buttons on my guitar.

He teaches me the basics, how to play the green, red and yellow notes on the easy level of the game. How to hit them at just the right time. How to hit the strum bar at the same time too. I butcher my way through *Slow Ride* and *Hit Me with Your Best Shot*, getting booed at by the virtual audience, tossed off stage. So I dig in, like a batter at the plate, eyes fixated on the screen, feet planted firmly on the ground, index, middle and ring finger poised over the notes. Chris walks behind me, adjusts the strap a bit, moving the guitar a bit lower. He places his right hand on top of mine on the notes.

Damn. There goes my concentration. His hand feels so good. The slightest bit of contact with him turns me inside out. I'm not used to this feeling. I don't know what to do with this feeling. It doesn't fit in my life. It fits in a song, and I don't know how to make it fit for me.

"So this may sound cheesy, but the real key is to let go. Let go of the need to check where your hands are, or to look constantly at the neck of the guitar."

I nod.

"So what I want you to do is close your eyes."

"Close my eyes?"

"Yes, close your eyes. I know it's going to be real hard for you not to be in control for one second, but trust me."

"Oh, ha ha," I tease.

"Yes, McKenna. I've already picked up that you like to be in charge."

"You're astute."

"I am. Now do as I tell you. Close your eyes."

I do as he tells me.

"So you have to just *feel* where your fingers are. So here's the green note." He places his finger down on top of my index finger, playing the green note.

Mmm...

"Here's the red." He presses his middle finger against mine, playing the red note now. I want to lean into him, to fall against him, and feel his chest on my back. I want him to wrap his arms around me, and hold me tighter as he teaches me to play. I want to feel his touch. I want contact. I want it so badly, I don't know how I'll ever play a song because I am living and breathing only one thing right now – the wish to be closer to him, my back curved into his front, his arms wrapped tight around me, our bodies beginning to entwine.

"And here's the yellow." He keeps his ring finger against mine, playing the yellow note. Then he holds the note. His fingers are playing my fingers, and my entire body feels like a tuning fork, vibrating hotly from his touch. "So you want to *feel* the notes, not look at them. Just know when green comes up, your index finger presses down. When red appears, your middle finger. When yellow shows up, your ring finger."

I played arcade games for fun when I was a kid, for release when I was left curbside by my ex. But I have never used video games as foreplay. I have never known video games could be foreplay. Here with Chris in some semi-private room at an electronics store, of all places, it feels like foreplay. It feels like he could turn me around, place his hands on my cheeks, and pull me in for a kiss. The kind that makes the world fall away. That leaves you powerless to resist, helpless to do anything but be consumed with an endless kiss. Nothing else matters, and the kiss is all there is, all there was, all there will ever be.

Until it becomes more than a kiss. It becomes heat in your blood, and a roaring in your ears, and you have to clutch the guitar so you don't turn around and show your hand to him. Show it in your eyes, and in the way you part your lips, and in the words that threaten to tumble from your lips. Words like *I want you so much.*

Words I pin down inside me so they can't escape.

He leans in a little closer this time and nearly whispers in my ear. "You can open your eyes now."

I inhale deeply and open my eyes. I feel wobbly from the way he's touched me, from the way I've let my thoughts spin into a dark and dangerous place of possibility. It's one thing for me to visit with his mouth in my fantasies; it's entirely another to witness my thoughts spin wildly with him inches away. He grasps my shoulders so I don't fall. Then I press start on Poison's *Talk Dirty to Me.* I hit the green notes, then the red notes, then the yellow ones. Then the next set and the next. I even nail a long note, then another, then a whole sequence of so-called "star-power" notes, and I give in to the game. I channel all my desire right now into the playing, and I am jamming here, rocking out to a video game, the pseudo-music taking my mind off the fact that I want Chris to talk dirty to me.

I finish my first song. I raise my hands in the air. Victory.

Chris smiles, big and wide, the teacher proud of his student. "Fast learner are you," he says in Yoda's voice.

"You're a *Star Wars* geek too!"

He shrugs sheepishly. "You want to play some more?"

I nod vigorously and then spend the next hour knocking out several more songs and even making it through my very first guitar battle, where I own the guitarist from Rage Against the Machine after two tries. By the time we turn off the game, I am feeling pretty energized. So I buy my own used copy of the game and walk out of the store with Chris.

"Want to grab a bite to eat? I know a taco shop around here."

"Abso-fucking-lutely."

So I take him to a hole-in-the-wall taqueria, a true Mexican place, with orange Formica booths and countertops and a menu that's half-English, half-Spanish. We order chicken quesadillas to share and two Diet Cokes.

"I don't want you caffeinating alone," Chris says to me, as he carries the soda cans and two glasses back to the table.

"How gallant of you." He pushes a can toward me. I squeal inside with delight. He *didn't* open it for me. He didn't rob me of the soda-can-crack-open. He *is* gallant. I open my soda and pour it into a glass. He does the same with his.

"Gallant McCormick, that's what they called me in school."

"So where'd you grow up? Let me guess. San Diego? Since you have the whole California surfer look going on."

He shakes his head. "Brooklyn of all places, but I hate cold, so I got the hell out of town for college."

"Where was that?"

"Stanford."

"Stanford?"

Ha laughs. "What? Just because I'm not wearing a pocket protector or a business suit?"

"I didn't mean it like that. I just was surprised. I guess because you're so laid back. You're the video game guy, you're a hipster. You don't seem like a Stanford stiff."

"I studied software design."

"Wow. You know some serious shit."

"That I do."

"So what'd you do after college?"

"Got a job designing software for video games," he says. The waitress brings us the quesadillas. Chris says thanks and she leaves. "I did that for a couple years and then decided I wanted to do my own thing. So I started consulting, doing business strategy and whatnot for companies in the gaming space. Got asked to speak at conferences, then started video blogging, then the video blog turned into a TV show. And here we are now, me and my gaming empire."

"And here we are now, indeed."

"And you, McKenna Bell?"

I tell him my story, growing up in Sherman Oaks, college at UCLA, a few years at Violet Summers, the fashion brand, then launching The Fashion Hound with Todd's help, then the sale. "So there you go. You know my story. What's yours?"

"I just told you my story," he reminds me playfully. Then I feel him tapping my foot once, twice under the table. Is he playing footsie? Is this how flirting works?

My face turns red. I don't know what to say. I don't even know anymore what I meant when I said *what's your story*. How is it I can be so good at suggesting how to assemble outfits, but so bad at knowing how to interact with a handsome man?

"You mean am I involved with anyone?" he asks.

Fire engine red now. I am totally, one hundred percent fire engine red. Was I that obvious?

110

"Sure," I manage to say, but the word comes out all choppy, as if it has ten syllables.

He shakes his head. "No."

I fight the urge to grin broadly like the Cheshire Cat.

"But you, you've got men all over," Chris adds.

*Yes, but you're the one I really want to date. If only you were twenty-three….*Why did I have to take that oath with my girlfriends? You can't break a girlfriend oath. That's like fifty years of bad luck if you do. Not to mention it's against the code. I can't go against the girl code, no matter how much I want to forget Trophy Husbands right now, and focus only on how the heck I can date this one guy.

"I narrowed the candidates down to about twenty of your guys and then my brain just stopped. I couldn't figure out how to weed them down to some sort of reasonable number."

But none of those twenty are as devastatingly handsome as you.

He shakes his head, amused at my predicament, then lays his hands on the table. "Have your viewers vote on the top five."

My eyes widen. "Chris! That is a great idea. That's really perfect. It involves viewers more. Makes them feel more vested in the show. Gives them a voice."

"Exactly. They feel a part of it. They *are* a part of it. They will have had a role, a hand, in picking your next mate. You can even have them decide who gets a second date and so on. You can shoot video of the dates and post clips and let them choose."

"I love it! It becomes even more of an interactive show." I point at him a few times, shaking my head appreciatively. "You rock," I say, wishing he could be one of the twenty, one of the five. And then I could date him. And dating him wouldn't be political, it wouldn't be to get even, it wouldn't be to make a point. It would be for the simplest of reasons. Because I want to.

He smiles back at me, his sea-green eyes sparkling. I think again of Hawaii, of a beach, of a secluded island cove when I look into them. For a second, I feel like I am being hypnotized. Maybe I actually am. Because I can't seem to take my eyes off of him. I can't seem to break the gaze, nor can he, and now he's looking at me in this more intense way, not just the flirty way, but in a way that takes my breath away. A way that says I wasn't wrong, I wasn't crazy, I wasn't delusional for thinking there were unsaid things at lunch. He looks at me as if he wants to know me, wants to see inside me, wants me to open up to him. And that's when it occurs to me. That's when everything comes together in one crystal-clear blaze of brilliance.

Business. I am good at business. So I keep it on the business level.

I lower my voice. "Chris, I have a fabulous business idea. I think you should be one of the initial twenty."

He laughs, kind of surprised. "You're not serious. Are you?"

I nod several times. "This is a business proposition pure and simple. You're a businessman and I'm a businesswoman, right?"

"Right."

"And you are trying to reach girl gamers for your show. You said that two days ago. Well, let's do more than a promo. Let's make you a candidate. You said your Wikipedia page has you at twenty-three anyway. So you could be twenty-three, you can pass for it, and obviously viewers will vote for you. They'll pick you as one of the five to date. And then you'll be on my show in a bigger way than just a promo. You'll be a contender. You know as well as I do that brand integration is the way to go."

"I love it when you talk dirty, McKenna."

"You know it's true," I say emphatically. "You become part of the Trophy Husband project, then my viewers will get to know you, they'll check out your show, they'll check out you and bam. You are well on your path as you reach out to female gamers."

"Okay," he says slowly. "I like the way you're thinking. I like everything you're saying. And yes, I do need to get the word out about my new show. But there's one teensy, tiny little problem." He holds up his thumb and index finger to show a small amount of space.

"What's that?"

He holds up his hands, as if to protect himself. "Now, this isn't personal. This isn't about you. But, I don't want to be a Trophy Husband."

I give him a look. A look that says *you can't be serious*. A look that rebuilds my barriers and protects me from letting him see too far into me, into the truth of this business deal. That it's not merely for business. But that the game might be the only way I can move closer to him without revealing all that I feel for him. In my body and in my heart. "Chris, this is a business deal. You and I are business partners. I am not asking you to move in, I am not asking you to be my man, I am not even asking you to be my boyfriend," I say, deliberately not adding *husband* to the list. I make a mental note of the fact that I can't even breathe the word *husband*, let alone bear to utter it.

"But I kind of thought that was what this contest was all about."

"Yes and no. It's about proving a point," I say, returning to my platform, like a politician. My talking points. Because the more he questions me, the more I lose sight of my goals. The more I lose sight of the game. Because there's no game with him whatsoever. Everything I feel for him is so scarily real, but I can't let him know that though.

"So you're not actually going to go through with this? The marriage thing?"

113

"All I want to do is prove that a woman can play a man's game. So play with me. It makes things interesting to have you on the show." I pause, then continue. "This is the Web. People want to laugh, they want to be entertained. They want to see people do wild things they can't do on regular TV. They want us to be daring. They want us to do the things they can't do."

Chris shifts back and forth a bit, considering.

I go for the kill. "And you like to play games. C'mon, you're a gamer, Chris. This is the ultimate game. Come on my show and play my game and let's see if you can win."

"Oh, those are fighting words that cut straight to my competitive heart."

"Good. I knew I could hook you that way."

"So you want me to be your pretend boy toy for the sake of making a point?"

"Dude, I totally want to make a point with you."

"Now it does sound like you're talking dirty to me."

I quirk up my lips and I'm not sure what comes over me, but maybe it's the fact that I've already had his hands on me, his mouth on me, that in my fantasies he knows what I taste like. So I say, "Maybe I am."

Chris rises and switches sides, sliding into the booth next to me. My heart leaps into my throat. My belly does a flip flop, and I am warm all over. Wait, make that white-hot when he fingers a strand of my long hair, playing with it. Does he have any idea what he does to me? Can he tell that I want to be tangled up in his arms? That I want to him to move me under him, to slide inside me, to lay his hot body on mine as he takes me? "You know, if I'm going to be a candidate, I think it's only fitting, don't you think, for me to kiss you?"

"You mean to sort of test the waters?"

"Make sure we're a good fit."

114

"So this would be like a business partner kiss?"

"Since we're in business together, yes."

"Then this would be a business kiss."

"All business."

"Okay, Chris. You may business kiss me now."

His hand finds its way to the back of my neck and the feeling of his firm hand on me makes me shudder. I close my eyes reflexively, letting myself feel that little zing that rushes from my belly down to my toes and back up again, as he leans into me, his soft lips brushing mine, his hand still gently resting on my neck, his fingers playing with my hair. It's not a long kiss, just a few seconds, but enough time for me to notice his lips are soft and full, his breath tastes fresh, and that even a even a starter kiss from him feels a bit like magic and music and falling all in one. He pulls away slowly, his lips taking their time leaving mine.

It's better than all my fantasies. It's ten million times better. Because it's real, and it's tangible, and it's happening, and he's touched me, and I want so much more. I want him. All of him.

I am an open book now – my lips parted slightly, hoping for more, my shoulders rising and falling. My eyes telling the truth, I am sure. He has to know. He has to know this is more with him. That this can be everything.

As he breaks the kiss, the look on his face says he liked it, and he wants so much more. I recognize the look, because I'm sure I'm his mirror image right now.

Plus, now I can date Chris.

Chapter Eleven

"She's been fed and she had an afternoon walk, but if you can take her out for twenty minutes when you stop by, that would be great."

I gather my purse and keys as I finish up the instructions with Ms. Pac-Man's regular dog-sitter/dog walker/dog trainer. I hired Wednesday Logan when we adopted Ms. Pac-Man and I'm also the one who attended every dog training session and implemented the instructions. But who's counting? Oh, wait. I am.

"Can you be sure to leave an invoice for me on the kitchen table?" I add as we chat on the phone. "I left cash for you already, but if you can leave an invoice that would be great."

"Absolutely," Wednesday says. "I can't wait to see Ms. Pac-Man again."

"And don't forget if you run into Michelangelo, stay far away."

"The horny pug, right?"

"Yep. She growls at him every time. But it's totally his fault. He tried to hump her once and she's not into that."

"Of course not. She's a lady dog."

"Exactly."

I end the call and meet Hayden to catch a bus to Fillmore, since Julia has decided we need a Girls Night Out and we're meeting her at the Tiki Bar, a loungy-bar with tapas and big, fiery drinks. She said the place is usually packed with young, hot men in their early twenties.

I'm wearing my new V-neck *Macbeth* shirt, a short flowy skirt, and a pair of red heels with a buckle strap. The whole ensemble can be had for under $100 and I shared the shopping details with my viewers last week. Our stop is a few blocks away from The Tiki Bar, so we get off the bus and walk the rest of the way. My phone chirps from my purse and I answer it.

"Hey, it's Chris."

"Hey there. What's going on?"

Hayden instantly looks back at me. She might as well have boy radar. She can glean within nanoseconds when you're talking to a guy. Well, any good girlfriend can. It's in our DNA. It's a requirement.

"So I guess if we're really going to be partners in crime, I need to send you a photo to post, huh?"

"Of course. You have to play by the rules."

We cross the street, Hayden deliberately staying two steps ahead. This pace is part of our DNA too; we are genetically programmed to give a fellow girlfriend the two-step spread during guy calls.

"Rules. I do well with rules," he says, and his voice is super flirty, and it makes me feel melty.

I adopt a sharp but playful tone. "The rule then is you need to send a picture soon. I announced yesterday on the show that I am posting pictures tomorrow night for voting."

"Oooh, giving me orders already. I like that. Makes me feel like a boy toy."

"Better watch out, Chris. Soon, I may be asking you to arrive at my house and pretend to be the pool boy."

"I could totally do a cabana boy look for you."

"If I had horses you could be a stable boy."

"Giddy up."

I laugh, and so does he, and the sexy banter makes me feel, for a moment, as if Todd might not be the last word in my life when it comes to men. Then I tell myself to settle down. We've only had one kiss, and besides, this is all just a game.

He's a gamer, and his competitive instincts are firing on all cylinders. That's all this is.

I see the Tiki Bar just ahead. The code dictates you must complete all phone calls to guys before entering the appointed location for a girls' night out. Phone conversations are only permitted in the window of time immediately before entering the establishment, and phone loitering is specifically forbidden.

"Hey, Chris. I have to go. It's girl's night out, so let me call you later."

"Enough said. Talk to you later."

"Who was that?" Hayden asks, as we walk inside The Tiki Bar, but it's noisy, and there's a part of me that's afraid of saying the truth out loud – that was the guy I'm majorly crushing on. Because if I voice those words, they become real. If I keep it to myself, maybe I can protect myself from heartbreak, so I pretend I didn't hear her as we make our way to my sister. Besides, they want this for me. They want me to see this Trophy Husband quest all the way through. Julia is already holding court at a corner table, a garish pink drink with not one, but two umbrellas in front of her. It's ironic, her drinking this, and she knows it. She, the uber-cool bartender, is drinking a strawberry daiquiri because it's an ironic act.

She's collected two boys, one on each side. "Look! I'm recruiting for you."

"I thought it was a girl's night out."

118

"And on a girl's night out, we like to meet boys. C'mon! The more the merrier when it comes to trophies! Let's see who we have in store for you tonight."

I do my best to push Chris from my mind and focus on my turn-the-tables project. I slide in next to Boy Number One, who sports a buzz cut, broad shoulders, and a white-and-green-striped button-down shirt. Julia introduces him as Carl. Bachelor Number Two flanks her other side. He's Tom, a little on the short side, but with warm brown eyes. They both smile.

We exchange pleasantries and admire Julia's drink, and then Julia gets down to business. She leans forward, laying her palms flat against the uneven wood table, warped with the sloshed juice of spilled drinks over the years. "So listen," she begins, eyeing the boys. "My hot sister is looking for a young man to be a *kept* man. There's like this big contest going on, I mean this is better than *American Idol*. This is your meal ticket, Tom and Carl."

I do my best not to roll my eyes. Julia could be in sales. The boys are enrapt, though that could be her lush auburn hair or the low-cut pink top she's wearing. Then Julia snaps a finger at Hayden, who reaches into a black suede bag. She extracts a thick stack of business cards, the kind you print yourself, the perforated edge as the tell-tale sign of the do-it-yourselfer.

"Shut up!" I say to Hayden. I had no idea she was up to something.

"I told you that if you're in this, we're in this with you. So we thought we'd do a little grassroots marketing for you. Think of us as your on-the-ground Skyy Vodka girls," Hayden says.

I reach for a card and read. "Have you ever dreamed of doing nothing all day but looking good and servicing your woman? Then sign up for the Trophy Husband Sweepstakes. Your chance to be a kept man. Every boy's dream."

I look at Julia, then Hayden. "Sweepstakes? Is this a sweepstakes now?"

Julia rolls her eyes. "Hello? It's like the biggest sweepstakes there is."

The thought flickers through my mind that this thing is taking on a life of its own. Calling the quest a "sweepstakes?" This has gone well beyond little old me. It's like a bullet train, hurtling through town after town, picking up passengers, gaining speed. I might as well be hosting a reality show online, a contest for my next mate.

Then again, that kind of is what I am doing, letting viewers pick the dates. Earlier in the week, the national talk show host Helen even mentioned my pursuit on air.

So we pass out cards, and chat up guys, and the whole thing has an air of crazy fun, and I suppose it has to, because I know in some ways I have to keep a distance from the reality of it. I prefer the unreality of the contest. But even as I talk to other guys, I'm only thinking about one guy. The one who called. The one who kissed me. The one I wouldn't mind seeing again.

"Where's Erin? She's supposed to be meeting us," Hayden shouts, and I reach for my phone and send Erin a quick text: *Hey, you going to join us for this girls night out or what?*

I lay my phone on the table and seconds later, it buzzes. I click on the envelope icon. But it's not from Erin. It's from Chris. Turns out I didn't write to Erin. I wrote to Chris accidentally since his was the last call I received, Erin's the second to last.

Tempted, but I am pretty sure my presence is verboten. Where, may I ask, are the festivities?

"What'd she say?" Hayden asks, peering through her tortoise-shell glasses to try to read the message.

"Not Erin," I say, as I quickly type a response: *So sorry, meant to write to my girlfriend Erin. We're on Fillmore.* I pause for a second, wondering where he lives, wondering if I should ask. After all, he managed to weave in a question in his text message. That's what you do when you want the volley to continue. So I add: *What are you up to?*

I hit send. Then I click back to the main screen and look at Hayden and Julia. "Are you all done with your messaging now? You think you can focus on us?" Hayden asks.

"Um, yeah," I say, feeling a little sheepish. I don't like when people spend more time on their phones than with the actual company they're keeping. I've always believed in focusing on real people and not the electronic tethers to what I might be missing, like Chris, who is somewhere in this city, somewhere near me…

I shake my head, clearing my thoughts, restoring a tabula rasa to my brain. I may have a wicked crush on him, but I can't let myself get swept up. The viewers might not choose him. They might not vote for him as one of the five finalists. Besides, we're business partners trying to grow our shows. That's all. We're playing a game, nothing more.

Erin comes rushing in, a torrent of energy, decked out in tight black jeans, a pink and gray argyle short-sleeve sweater and gigantic pink plastic earrings in the shape of squares. She sits down in a huff, pushes a hand through her spiky hair, and says, "I need a drink. You will never believe what happened to me tonight."

She motions to the waiter and orders a vodka straight up. "My VIP client wanted a happy ending."

"What?" I say, shocked.

"A happy ending. He asked for a happy ending. Does he think we're running a fucking bordello?"

"Jesus, Erin. Why would he do that?"

"Evidently, one of the other girls, *Karen*, has been giving him happy endings, that's why. So when he booked for tonight, the receptionist didn't hear him right when he made his special request for Karen." The waiter, exceedingly prompt, returns with Erin's drink. She reaches for it instantly and downs about half the glass. "So she assumed it was me because our names sound similar. Anyway, so as I finish the massage, he taps his hip. I pretend I don't see it. He taps his hip again and says, 'Karen always finishes me off. Can you?'"

She takes another drink, then practically slams her glass down.

"Ugh. That is so gross," Julia says.

We commiserate with her for a few more minutes, and then Julia regales us with her craziest work stories, and soon Erin has downed another glass.

I excuse myself for the restroom. Once inside, I reach for my phone again. I don't want them to know I'm texting with Chris. Not when they're having such a good time playing the game too. Besides, Chris is just playing the game as well, I tell myself. I can't let myself get too fixated on one guy, even though I want to. Especially since there's a new message from him, and his name alone on my screen thrills me. *Testing out the new Ajax Extra car racing game. It sucks...Where are the girls tonight?*

He asked me another question. He likes chatting with me. And I like chatting with him so much it's starting to scare me. But in a good way. In the way that makes my mouth curve into a smile and my skin tingle.

We're making the rounds on Fillmore Street. What part of the city do you live in?

I hit send, tuck the phone in my purse and return to Erin. During my short bathroom trip, she's managed to acquire another vodka and she's quickly necking this one back.

Then we leave and we blanket nearby bars, laughing like college girls playing pranks, as we hand out Trophy Husband flyers at The Pink Pantry, Cosmo Pete's, Akimbo and Car 282. People are getting a kick out of the contest, saying they love how it turns the tables. That's the point, and I love it when people get the point I'm making.

But I am also feeling pretty good because Chris and I have been texting all night. And even though I've only consumed two beers in two hours, his notes are giving me a little buzz of their own.

Erin, however, has been drinking enough for the four of us. I lost count of how many she's polished off. She's pretty sloshed, laughing her ass off at nearly everything and bobbing and weaving as she heads to the restroom, now that we're back at our home base of the Tiki Bar, mission accomplished many times over.

"What are we going to do about her?" Hayden asks, pointing to the ladies room. "She drove here from work."

"We need to take her home, obviously."

"I need to head back anyway since Lena will be up at the crack of dawn tomorrow. So we'll all just catch a cab and drop her off?"

"Yeah, and I guess she'll just get her car tomorrow," I say, then reach into my purse once more when I feel my phone vibrate. The girls are chatting amongst themselves now, so I figure I can get away with a quick reply to Chris. Provided it's Chris. I hope it's Chris. *How's the night going? Will it be an all nighter?*

I tap back: *Wrapping up soon. What are you doing?*

The girls chatter more. Chris replies almost instantly.

Closing shop for the night. No more games. I'm ready for more rules. You?

Rules? Is he asking to see me? I glance quickly at my friends, then at Erin, zigzagging her way back to the table, her eyes a little loopy from the liquor.

She plops down, resting her head on my shoulder. I pet her short, spiky hair. "Hey, babe. We're all going to share a cab and get you home safely."

She springs up. "What about my car?" She's got a look of sheer terror in her eyes.

"Erin, we'll come get it tomorrow."

She shakes her head emphatically. "No, no, no. Pete will freak out if I leave the car on Fillmore overnight. He's always worried that cars will be towed or vandalized."

"Erin, are you nuts? Pete will be fine with the car."

"No, no, no," she says again, adamant. Then she looks at me with big puppy dog eyes. "Please, McKenna. Please take my car home tonight. You have a two-car garage. Please. You're not drunk. Please drive my car home. Please."

"Erin," I say patiently. "Sweetie, I had two drinks. I can't drive for another hour."

"Take it home in an hour then, please?"

Then it hits me. *Rules. Hour. You.* I hold up a finger, telling Erin to wait. I reach for my phone again, tapping back a reply. *Can you meet me at Tiki Bar in 15 minutes?* I'm still not even sure he was asking me for a drink. But I'm seizing the moment. I'm making the most of my night out before a heavy week of dating starts. His yes arrives seconds later. So I help hail a cab for Hayden and Erin, then wait for another one for Julia since she lives in the opposite direction.

"It's just you and me, sis," Julia says, looping her arm through mine.

Uh oh. I thought Julia was leaving too. "Um, Julia," I begin, feeling my face turning red as I try to think of ways to politely ask her to get the hell out of here.

She looks at me, wide-eyed, her jaw open, seeing right through me. She pokes my chest. "You're meeting a boy!"

"No," I say quickly. Then I change my tune. "Actually, yes."

She holds up a hand for a high-five. "You work fast!"

"Actually. He's that video game guy. You know the one who talked up my show last week and sent all those guys to me?"

Julia gives me a quizzical look. "He's twenty-three?"

"Yeah, can you believe it?"

"Weird, he seemed more like our age. But cool. He wants in on the action?"

"Um, yeah, as it turns out. He's a fun guy, liked the contest, so he wanted to join in too."

"But I thought you were saying he kind of ran a big video game empire or something?"

What is this – Twenty Questions?

"Yeah. So?"

"I just figured a Trophy Husband doesn't work. You know, because trophy wives don't work. But heck, what do I know? You're making the rules up as you go along, you're a pioneer! You're blazing a trail to a world teeming with Trophy Husbands!"

"That's me. The pioneer," I say dryly.

She wags a finger at me. "Just remember. Twenty-three and under. Only younger guys."

"Totally. Of course. I took the oath. I'd never break it."

"You better not." She raises her hand and waves frantically at a nearby cab.

"I won't," I say with a fake smile. I have just lied to my sister, to my awesome amazing sister who I love. I have just lied to her face about Chris' age. About the oath I took. The girlfriend oath that I'm breaking. Then, I remind myself that Chris is not going to be the winner. This little thing we have going on is a business deal, a promotional partnership. It's a game. That's all it is. A game. Still, I feel a little creepy, a little conniving for telling a lie.

A taxi pulls up.

"Have fun with video game guy. And hey, you're driving. So order a Diet Coke, okay?"

"Obviously. Diet Coke and me, we're like this," I say as I twist my index and middle fingers together.

She gives me a quick kiss and a hug, and then I return to where the evening started. When I walk back in Chris is sitting at the table in the corner, smiling at me. All my icky feelings fade.

Chapter Twelve

"So is this like an officially sanctioned date?" Chris asks playfully after the waitress brings us two Diet Cokes.

I press a finger to my lips. "Shh…"

"So this date is off the record then?"

"A secret date," I whisper. "A secret *business* date with the first Trophy Husband candidate."

"We don't even know if I'll make the cut."

"You will so make the cut. How could you not?"

"The odds are one in four, McKenna. And that's just for the first round, for the initial date."

"You'll get there. I'm not worried."

"I guess I'm getting a leg up on the others right now."

"You are indeed."

"Speaking of legs up, I was thinking we should still probably shoot that promo."

"Really? Why?"

"One, I have access to the studio and my videographer is on retainer with the network show so it won't cost us anything. And two, it's sort of like a fallback. What if I don't make the cut?"

"You will!"

"But, just in case. And, even if I am one of the five, your viewers might not pick me for a second date. So, we'd have to resort to the old-fashioned way to keep promoting each other, with promos, know what I mean? Because I definitely think there are great synergies between our shows –"

I cut him off. "Did you actually just say *synergies*?"

He rolls his eyes, aware of his faux pas. "Fuck, I did."

"That is like the ultimate corporate marketing term."

"I know, I know. That is so embarrassing," he says, then pauses. "But, it's not nearly as embarrassing as you not having played Guitar Hero until two days ago. I mean, I had to teach you a game they don't even make any more."

"What can I say? I'm a throwback. I like vintage tees and old standards for music."

"What's your favorite old standard ever?"

"Ever? As in all time?"

"Well, yeah. That would be ever."

"It's totally cheesy. You'll laugh."

"Try me."

I take a deep breath. "Can't Help Falling in Love by Elvis."

He doesn't say anything for a few seconds, and I tense. Have I scared him? Does he think that means I'm some crazy, clingy girl?

Then he leans into me, and presses his forehead against mine. He is so damn cute, it's killing me. "That is an awesome song," he says in a soft voice, and I can barely take it anymore, being this close to him. I want him to kiss me again so badly, it's like an ache that longs to be soothed. I want him to run his hands in my hair, to pull me closer, to savor my lips on his. The desire to be near him is so overwhelming that it's fogging my brain, and all I'm seeing, thinking, feeling is this wish to erase any distance between us. I have to pull away. If I stay any closer, I will fall into his arms, and God only knows what kind of hurt I'd be setting myself up for.

"So yeah, let's shoot a promo this week," I say, and like that – now you see it, now you don't – I am back-to-business McKenna.

We spend the next fifteen minutes sketching out ideas, then we move on to other topics, trading tales from college, telling stories of favorite concerts we have been to. He loves live music and tells me he has been to 227 concerts in his life.

"You count?"

He nods proudly.

"You actually count?"

"I keep a piece of paper in my desk listing every concert I have ever been to."

"Why?"

"It's the engineer in me, McKenna. What can I say? I like to count, to keep track of things."

"I so need to get a hold of that piece of paper."

"And for that I am keeping my desk under lock and key when you come over."

"Hey, where do you live? You never told me."

"Russian Hill. Corner of Polk and Green."

"I love that neighborhood. There is a great little kitschy gift shop a few blocks north on Polk Street where I got this ring," I say, then hold out my right hand. A silver band with pink and white flowers etched on it is on my index finger. A half dozen thin black plastic bangles rattle a bit on my wrist. Chris reaches for my hand, gently touching the ring. His fingertips graze the top of my hand as he moves along from my finger to my wrist, touching my bracelets now. I am hypnotized with his touch, tugged into an orbit around him, because he is the focal point of my body and mind right now. His hands are strong and soft and they make my skin warm all over, as if I've been lying out in the sun, soaking in the delicious rays. He strokes the inside of my wrist so briefly, but enough for a tiny whimper to escape my lips as my mind flashes forward to other things he might be able to do with his hand. I press my thighs together, so I don't grab his hands and test my theories.

"You know, McKenna," he says, rubbing his thumb and forefinger along one of my bangles. For a second, I think he's going to say something about my penchant for accessories. But instead, he kind of nods at my tee-shirt, at the crown hanging off the last letter in the name of the "Scottish Play."

"You have cool tee-shirts."

I laugh a little.

"I noticed that about you the first time I met you."

"You did?" I ask, not in a questioning way, but to keep up the conversation.

"That time at the electronics store, the first thing I noticed was you were hot. The second thing I noticed was you were funny. The third thing I noticed was you were really cool. And the fourth thing I noticed was you had on this cool tee-shirt with a squirrel waterskiing on it. I like a chick with a good tee-shirt collection."

I smile. Or maybe I beam. Because I don't know which of those four things I like better – being thought of as hot, funny, cool or stylish. I like them all, for different reasons, but I have to say he saved the best for last. He likes my tee-shirts, he likes my style. He likes what makes me me, and that's enough for me to feel totally under his spell, body and heart.

"No one has ever said that to me," I say with a smile, pushing my hair back, leaning my head a little to the side, deliberately flirting with him. I am doing those things behavioral scientists say men and women do when they write their "Science of Flirting" articles: sit closer, make eye contact, flick their hair. I am the "Science of Flirting" right now and I don't care. I'm not flirting because he's a contender, I'm not flirting because he's my partner in crime. I'm flirting because I want to. And I am pretty sure when Chris smiles back at me, a sparkle in his eyes, that he's flirting for the same reasons. I linger on his eyes for a moment, his Hawaii eyes, pools of green that strip me bare with the way he looks at me when his playfulness shifts to intensity.

Then I break the gaze because it's getting late. "I should get going. My dog probably misses me."

He pays the bill. "Since this wasn't an official date, I'm going to skirt the Trophy Husband rules and be the gentleman here."

We head out of the Tiki Bar and walk slowly up Fillmore. At the top of the hill, I see Erin's maroon Prius. I point to it.

"These are my wheels." I click on the key to unlock the car. Then I reach for the door handle. But it doesn't open. I try again. Same thing happens. "Damn. What is up with these hybrids?"

"They have to calibrate to your heart rate."

"Then how the heck am I supposed to drive it home?"

"I know a trick," Chris says.

"You do?"

"Remember, McKenna, I'm a software engineer by training."

"Software engineer. Car burglar. They're practically the same thing these days," I say, as I turn to face him.

"Want to give me the keys and I'll show you?" he asks, holding open his palm for me.

But before I can pull away, he closes his fingers over mine, gripping my hand in his. That's all it takes. Within seconds I am in his arms, and we are wrapped up in each other. His lips are sweeping mine, and I press my hands against his chest, and oh my. He does have the most fantastic outlines in his body. He is toned everywhere, strong everywhere, and I am dying to get my hands up his shirt, and feel his bare chest and his belly. But if I did, I might just jump him right here because I am one year and running without this. Without kissing, without touching, without feeling this kind of heat.

He twines his fingers through my hair, and the way he holds me, both tender and full of want at the same time, makes me start to believe in possibilities. Start to believe that you can try again, and it'll be worth it. His lips are so soft, so unbearably soft, and I can't stop kissing him. He has the faintest taste of Diet Coke on his lips, and it's crazy to say this, but it almost makes me feel closer to him. Or maybe I feel closer because he's leaning into me, his body is aligned with mine, and there's no space between us, and I don't want any space between us. I want to feel him against me, his long, strong body tangled up in mine, even though we're fully clothed, making out on the street. I don't know how it happened, but somewhere along the way I've grabbed his tee-shirt, my fingers curled tightly around the fabric.

He breaks the kiss, but I don't let go of his clothes. I don't let go of him. "I wanted to kiss you all night."

"You did?"

"Yeah, that key thing was just an excuse. Sometimes you just have to hit the button a few times to get the car to open."

I laugh. "So you said that to kiss me?"

He nods. "Totally."

"I'm glad you tricked me," I whisper, as he bends his head and kisses my neck, blazing a trail of sweet and sexy kisses down to my throat, and it's almost sensory overload the way he ignites me. Forget tingles, forget goosebumps. That's kid stuff compared to this. My body is a comet with Chris. I am a shooting star with the way he kisses me. I don't even know if I have bones in my body anymore. I don't know how I'm standing. I could melt under the sweet heat of his lips that are now tracing a line down my chest to the very top of my breasts, as he tugs gently at my shirt, giving himself room to leave one more brush of his lips, before he stops.

He looks at me, and the expression on his face is one of pride and lust. He knows he's turned me inside out and all the way on.

"That was so unfair of me," he says with a wicked grin, as I finally loosen the grip on his shirt. The fabric is wrinkled in the middle of his chest, marked by my need to hold him close. "Getting a headstart like that on all the other candidates."

How can there be any other guys after a kiss like that? It's a kiss to end all kisses, it's a sip of lemonade in a hammock on a warm summer day. It's a slow dance on hardwood floors while a fan goes round overhead, curtains blowing gently in the open window.

If he feels half as much for me as I do for him, then I want to sail away with him in the moonlight, and that scares the hell out of me. I have to extract myself before I let this go any further. I don't mean the contact. I mean the way my aching, broken heart is reaching for Chris.

I channel my business self. My other side. The strong, tough side that won't be hurt ever again.

"I should go," I say.

Then he clicks on the car opener and I hear the doors unlock. He opens the door for me and I slip into the front seat. He's about to close the door when I say, "Do you want me give you a ride home?"

He shakes his head.

"But Russian Hill is at least a couple miles from here. Let me drive you."

"I'll walk. I like the city at night." Then he leans in to me, gently pushes my hair back and looks at me with a truly devilish smirk, his green eyes twinkling. "Besides, if I got into that car with you I wouldn't be able to keep my hands off of you. And we all know that really wouldn't be fair to the others."

"My, aren't you considerate," I say, keeping it light. "Goodnight, Chris."

"Goodnight, McKenna."

Then I drive away, watching Chris begin his long walk home in my rearview mirror. I head down Fillmore Street toward the water and he's no longer a speck in the distance.

He's gone.

* * *

As I drive back to the Marina, I do what girls, what women, always do in these moments. I replay the kiss. I put it on repeat in my mind. The way he grazed my neck with his hand, the way he lingered on a strand or two of hair, stroking it, touching it, like the shy but sexy Spanish guy did to Laura Linney in *Love, Actually* the night of the Christmas Party. She went wild inside, shivering with delight. I feel the same. I want to pull over on the side of the road. Pull over and lean my head back and close my eyes and just remember. But I keep driving, wriggling a bit in my seat as I find myself getting more turned on, getting wetter, the more I think about Chris, the more I think about what might have happened in this car if he'd taken me up on my offer for a ride home. I think about rolling up to a stop sign somewhere on a quiet street and going for another kiss. Then stopping on the side of the road and turning off the engine, then the lights, then climbing into his seat and making out in a parked car, a friend's car no less, as he kisses me more. The kind of kiss where I let go, where I breathe out his name in a long, slow, lingering sigh that borders on a prayer. The kind of kiss that winds down my body, lips against my belly, fingertips grazing my waist. That makes me want to rock my hips into him, to let him take me places I haven't been, as I let him inside me, all the way in. And when he's there, it feels so right, so good, so deliriously out-of-this-world, that all I can do is say his name in a breathless, ragged kind of whisper as I struggle to form words because all the things he does have made me come undone for him.

Like a good boyfriend would do.

As I pull into my own garage I am struck by a simple thought: it would be kind of nice right now just to have a boyfriend, just a boyfriend, nothing more.

Chapter Thirteen

I don't usually have questions about whether to fight or flight. I'm almost always on the side of fight. But when I see Amber a few days later power walking with her baby strapped to her chest, all I want to do is flee.

Because Amber is the living, breathing manifestation of all that I never was.

Good enough to keep a man walking all the way down the aisle.

She had something I never had. I don't even know what it is about her. Is it her looks, all hourglass redhead? Or is it her body and the way she can bend? Or it is more? Is she funnier, smarter, more interesting? Does she love harder, better, more? How did he know in one night that he wanted to be with her forever?

I don't have those answers as I walk my dog along the Marina bike path on a weekday morning. I don't think I'll ever have those answers. Worse, I don't know if I'll ever stop wanting them. It's like there's this raw wound inside me that can never be exposed to enough air to heal. I'll never be able to treat it, so it'll become a part of me, the ulcer in my heart that won't ever go away.

And that's why I want to duck and hide right now, to roll into a bush and curl up with my dog, like we're two soldiers who've found a foxhole for protection.

But she sees me, and she waves and smiles.

Breathe deeply. Turn over a new leaf. I am Zen McKenna. I am cool, calm and collected McKenna, as I walk in her direction, imagining I am a guru, a yoga instructor, a therapist. I am serene, I am graceful, I am a mountain breeze.

"Hey, McKenna," she says and stops.

Okay, so I guess I have to stop now too. But I don't have to be nice because I'm not a yoga instructor or a therapist. I'm the jilted and I don't like that the jilter is on my territory. "What are you doing in the city? Don't you live in the suburbs?"

Amber pats the back of the sleeping baby on her chest. "I started teaching again. Gymnastics. I have a class with two-year-olds in about a half hour over in the Marina with some of the mommies there."

"Oh, that is so sweet," I say and somehow find the restraint not to fake gag.

"I love teaching, and Charlotte is a good baby. She sleeps during the class. But I also just love being an independent woman and supporting our family."

"Oh," I say and place my hand on my chest as if I am so touched. "That's so lovely."

"It's important, don't you think? That's what your Trophy Husband quest is all about right? By the way, I love it. I love your show. And I just think we have to set examples. And mine is that I can be a working mom and help pay the bills."

"That's great," I say through gritted teeth.

"And how is sweet Ms. Pac-Man?"

Amber leans down to pet my dog, the sleeping baby angling close to my dog's face. I make a mental note to give the dog a bath when I return home. Then Ms. Pac-Man emits a low rumble. I snap my head and look at my dog. She's pulling back her doggy lips and showing her teeth.

I yank her collar and pull her away.

Amber stands at attention, a look of terror in her eyes.

I'm about to admonish my dog, who has never been anything but sweet with kids, when I realize she wasn't going after the baby. There's Michelangelo up ahead, trotting in our direction, his wrinkly little face and beige puggy body aiming straight for one of Ms. Pac-Man's legs.

A wicked sense of glee floods my veins. Because this isn't just parking karma. This is all the karma in the world.

"I'm so sorry about that, Amber. Todd must not have told you?"

"Told me what?"

"Oh. Yeah. Ms. Pac-Man doesn't like babies. Or kids for that matter. She growls at all of them. I'm working on it with her, but she's just not fond of the littles ones."

"Oh," Amber says and nods in understanding. "That's really good to know."

"Isn't it, though? All right, toodle-loo. I have to go."

Thank the lord for horny pugs.

* * *

"Here's my favorite part of dating. I get to do what I like best – devote my mental energy to assembling cute outfit combos," I say to the camera, then model the newest ensemble I'm wearing for an afternoon coffee chat. "Here's the worst part. You're caffeinated all the time. Because you constantly have to go out for coffee for first dates. I have never had so much coffee in my life."

We're shooting outside today, so I gesture to the coffee shop near my house, Your Other Office.

"So I'm just going to head in and grab another. After all, I have a date in, oh, about two hours. And guess what? It's Bachelor Number Four, thanks to you!" I point at the camera. "You know the drill. You picked 'em for me and I'm doing the dirty work, going on the dates. So, in two hours, I'll be reporting for duty and tomorrow, I'll report back so you can choose who deserves a second date. So keep voting, keep sharing your thoughts on the candidates. Because this isn't just about me. This is a communal effort, a collective Trophy Husband for all of us."

I salute the camera and give my usual sign-off. Then Andy turns off the camera and I sigh heavily. It's getting harder for me to keep up the act, but I don't want Andy to know.

"How was it?"

He gives a silent thumbs up. He packs up, staying quiet most of the time. I do my part, helping with the microphone, but decide to ignore his noiselessness. I counter it with chatter. "I'm exhausted."

He gives me a harrumph.

"What should I talk to this guy about?"

"Don't know," he says curtly.

"You want to just add a 'don't care' to the end of that statement?"

"What are you talking about?"

"I mean, that's kind of what you meant, right? *Don't know, don't care?*"

He stares at me for a second, then continues packing his camera gear.

"What is eating you?"

"You know what it is."

I do. The same thing that's eating away at Andy is what's been eating away at me since that kiss with Chris on Saturday night. Since then I've been going on the requisite dates with the top five, and, as I predicted, the viewers voted for Chris as one of the five. The dates are chaste, as they should be at this point in a dating contest, and nothing has happened physically with any of them. Chris is the only guy I've kissed and he's the only one I want to kiss. Even when I'm on other dates, my mind is on him. So I have to wonder if Andy's instincts are right.

I close my eyes, then press my thumb and forefinger against the corner of my eyelids, squeezing them, trying to find some sort of answer. But I don't even know what the question is and now my brain starts to hurt. I'm not in the mood for heavy reflection.

So I say goodbye to Andy and head to Your Other Office, trying to remember the name of the Trophy Husband candidate I'm meeting there soon. Craig? No, Craig was Monday's date. Craig and I had pizza at lunchtime sitting by the water. We grabbed slices at Martino's, a New York style pizzeria that uses the flimsiest paper plates possible. We walked a few blocks to the water, our plates sagging in the middle, grease threatening to spill out. We sat on the rocks just a few feet from the Bay, looking at the gorgeous Golden Gate Bridge. There is no more stunning bridge in the entire universe. I have lived in the Bay Area for six years and have never once grown tired of our rust-colored bridge. Its beauty always captures me, whether I'm driving across it, watching it from the ferry, or gazing at it. The Golden Gate Bridge *is* one of the wonders of the modern world. It is a marvel.

But Craig disagreed. "That is such an ugly bridge," he remarked as we sat down on the rocks. I choked on my pizza.

"What?" I said in between coughs.

"Man, if it were up to me I'd rip that sucker down," he said, casting a disdainful look toward the bridge.

"You're joking, right?"

He shook his head. "I'd make a sleek steel bridge. None of this suspension shit."

"Maybe you could tear down the Sistine Chapel, slash *The Nightwatch*, and see if you can get Shakespeare banned from school curriculum too."

Tuesday's boy was a little better, but still no prize. His name was Jared, he was a computer repair guy, and a major fan of Chris' show. But then all he did was talk about *Let the Wookie Win*. He told me he'd seen every episode twice. He told me he had added Chris to his Twitter account, so he got updates on Chris' online "status" throughout the day. He was vying to become one of Chris' "Top Friends" on Facebook, and could I do anything to help him achieve that goal?

I was already thinking of Chris the whole time during the date. With those constant mentions, it was as if Chris was running at a double-time loop in my brain.

As I walk into the coffee shop, I finally remember the name of today's date. Jean Paul Peter. I don't know his last name, but he has three first names. When he arrives, I switch on the iCam. The cards are all on the table now, so I'm going to share some of this date with the viewers. They'll be happy since Jean Paul Peter looks better than his picture. He's tall and built with lovely dark skin. He's wearing jeans and a long sleeve pullover, one that can't help but accentuate his sculpted arms. His hazel eyes are flecked with gold.

I stand up and shake his hand. "Pleasure to meet you, McKenna." Then he gestures to the counter. "May I get you a coffee, latte, hot chocolate?"

At the rate I'm plowing through caffeine, I'll be immune to the stuff pretty soon. He gets a latte, I order another coffee, and he carries them back to our chairs.

"I'm glad I made the cut," Jean Paul Peter begins.

"I'm glad you made the cut too, Jean Paul Peter."

He holds up a hand. "You can just call me JP."

I wipe my forehead in the mock "whew" gesture. "Jean Paul Peter is a mouthful of a name."

I spend the next thirty minutes chatting with JP. I learn that JP grew up in Florida, played football in high school, studied communications in college, and now at the ripe old age of twenty-two, he works as an assistant for a sports marketing firm. He's perfect. Truly perfect. He would be a perfect man for some woman.

"So JP, you're in sports marketing. What do you want to do with that?"

"Nothing really. I want to be a ski instructor. I try to go every weekend. Leaning in and out, speeding down the hill," he says, moving his sturdy frame a bit from side to side as if to demonstrate how to ski. "I would love to get a place in Tahoe and set up camp there and spend all day on the slopes, teaching people how to ski and skiing myself."

He wants a place in Tahoe. That means he wants me to get him a place in Tahoe. That's what the Sugar Daddies do for their ladies. They get them lakefront property, weekend getaways, houses in Hawaii. Apparently, that's what Trophy-Husbands-to-be expect from their Sugar Mamas too.

I realize for the first time that two people are playing the game. It's not just me taking Dave and Steely Dan Duran out for test drives, unbeknownst to them. Everything is on the table now. The candidates know the game is on and they're here because they want a meal ticket. I'm no longer the only one with requirements. They have their prerequisites too. JP wants a woman with money, a woman who can set him up, a woman who can make him a kept man so he can play on the slopes all day.

"So that's why you're in this contest, huh?"

"Excuse me?"

I strip the chit-chattery veneer away as I shut off the iCam. "To get a house in Tahoe, right? That's why you want to be a Trophy Husband?"

"Oh, that? Well, I like you, McKenna. I am having an excellent time with you. And I just believe in trying new things. And I thought this would be a fun way to meet someone."

"Someone who can set you up with a house in Tahoe?"

"Uh, well. You have always kind of said that you were looking for a kept man. And frankly I wouldn't mind being kept. So I thought I'd give this a shot."

"Right, of course."

I feel a momentary sense of kinship for the well-to-do older man who scouts out a trophy wife. Does he ever wonder if his woman is using him, if she only loves him for his money? Or maybe he doesn't care. Maybe I need to be more like a man and not care.

But I don't feel that way. I do care. I do care about someone. A lot.

And I have no idea what to do with these feelings. The last time I felt this way, I was about to walk down the aisle, and then went on to have my heart smashed.

* * *

The letter from Todd's lawyer arrives this afternoon. He is no longer contesting custody of the dog. I pump my fist in victory, but something about this feels empty. Or maybe it's just that I feel that way right now.

Empty.

Chapter Fourteen

There's a knock on my door. It's ten p.m.

These two facts should not occur simultaneously.

Fortunately, I have a dog who knows her job. Ms. Pac-Man emits a thunderous growl, then hits the repeat button on her vocal cords as she races to the front door, lifting her snout high in the air to express her displeasure at a late-night houseguest.

I stay low on my couch and wait for Ms. Pac-Man to stop. I make a mental note to buy her meat bones tomorrow as a reward for being the best guard dog. She keeps growling and then I hear a familiar voice over her practically lion-like roars.

"McKenna, it's Andy!"

I hop up from the couch, run downstairs, and open the door. I expect him to be all disheveled, maybe with a cut on his face or something. But he's normal Andy, dressed in jeans and a tee-shirt from Tokyo.

I hold my hands out. "Happy to see you, but what the hell are you doing banging on my door at ten o'clock?"

"Can I come in?"

I gesture for him to enter. He does. I shut the door.

"Diet Coke?"

He nods and follows me into the kitchen. I open the fridge and hand him a cool, cold can. I get one for myself too. He opens his, I open mine, and we stand there, like two gunfighters, caffeinated weapons at our side, waiting to draw.

"You scared the shit out of me. What can I do for you?"

"We have to talk."

"Okay."

"Look, I know I've been a jerk these last few weeks. But the fact is, I think you're better than all this Trophy Husband stuff."

I lean against the counter. "What do you mean?"

"You don't need a husband. You don't even need a boyfriend. You're amazing as is. I love working with you, and I love being your friend, and you're beautiful and smart and funny, and I hate watching you make a fool of yourself week after week."

"A fool?" I repeat. "I'm making a fool of myself week after week?"

Andy swallows and nods hard. "Yes, you are."

I put my hands on my hips. "And just how am I making a fool of myself?"

"Because you don't even like these guys. I watch the videos you send. I edit them. And I can tell you're not into them. The only time you ever seem interested is whenever you talk about that Video Game Guy. Chris."

I blush. It's as if I've been caught.

"So why are you still doing this?"

"Because…" Suddenly the words aren't coming to me. Suddenly the reasons are escaping me. Suddenly I am trying to tap into my well of anger and I am coming up dry. Maybe I have no more fight left.

"See?" Andy says, softly this time. He puts a hand on my shoulder. "You don't even know why you're doing this anymore." He reaches for my Diet Coke and hands it to me. "Take a drink."

I do as I'm told, enjoying a long, cold, bubbly gulp.

"I'm doing this because I want to show that women can do what men do. I want to even the score. I want to set things right."

"Right for who?"

"For everyone!"

"McKenna, it's over with Todd. He doesn't care what you do. He doesn't care if you prove him wrong. I doubt Amber cares either."

"It's not even about them anymore. I'm just trying to make a point," I say a little petulantly. As I do, I notice for the first time how ridiculous I sound.

"I just don't think this is a point worth making. Because this isn't just a point, McKenna. This is your life. It's not a game. It's not a show. It's your heart. You don't need a Trophy Husband to prove Todd was a dick for marrying Amber. Todd is a dick and nothing you ever do will disprove that. He will be a dick for time immemorial. He will go to his grave being a dick. The dude committed the ultimate crass and cruel act. But you know what? You don't have to find a husband on the Internet to prove you are better than a cheating scum! You *are* better than a cheating scum."

I run a hand through my hair, holding it tight against my scalp.

"Do you really want to marry JP or Joshua? Do you want to marry someone who wants to be a Trophy Husband? Someone who wants you because it's a fun game? Because you're loaded? Do you want someone who wants you for your money or for all that makes you totally fucking rock star fashion hound awesome?"

I don't answer at first because my instinct is to blow him off. To scoff. To hold up a hand and say *whatever*. But something about his questions have pierced their way through my Teflon. They've hit me inside, where it matters.

I've always seen a Trophy Husband as, well, to be honest – sort of like a little pet. Like a little pet I'd keep and feed and water and allow out on certain occasions. Not a person, not a lover, and maybe not even a friend. But that's what I really want. Someone who wants me for me. Someone who loves me for me. Someone who wants to take a chance on all that I am.

I look back at Andy. His eyes are sharp and focused, with so much passion in them. Passion as a friend. He's not here as my "employee." He's here, late at night, because he's my friend, and he cares. My throat hitches, because I'm so damn lucky to have friends who knock sense into me late at night. I didn't know how badly I needed this until he said those words. But I do. I do need this because I'm just doing the same thing I've done the last several months. I'm firing bullets at bad guys, when I should be tending to the wounds. Stitching up. Moving on.

"Do you even want a husband? Do you want to be married in a contest?"

"No," I croak quietly.

"I didn't hear you."

"No, Andy. I don't want to be married, I don't want a Trophy Husband, I want someone who loves me," I say, then I cover my eyes with my hand so Andy won't see that I'm starting to cry. But he can tell anyway, by the way my shoulders are shaking, so he pulls me against him. I bury my face in his tee-shirt. He pets my hair.

"Hey, it's okay. It's going to be okay"

"How is this going to be okay? How am I going to get myself out of this? What am I going to tell my girlfriends?"

"They love you, and so do your viewers. We'll figure it out."

"I am an idiot. I am a huge idiot."

"No, but you are the most pig-headed person I know."

"The most!"

"The absolute and most."

"The most pig-headed, hot-headed, stubborn person in all of San Francisco."

He scoffs. "In San Francisco? Try the world, baby"

I step away and reach for a tissue. I blow my nose. "I've made a big mess out of my life."

"Why don't you get some sleep and we'll figure this out on Monday, okay? Go on that date with the guy you like and we'll figure this out on Monday."

I nod and walk him to the door, then give him a hug.

On Monday I will go Gershwin & Gershwin in my video blog: *Let's Call the Whole Thing Off.* Yes, that's what I'll do. It'll be simple, it'll be easy. We can now return to our regularly scheduled programming. It'll be a piece of cake.

He leaves and I head to my living room, sinking down in the couch, feeling a strange sense of peace. I'm not the same ball of rage I've been. Anger doesn't feel as good anymore. I've grown weary of being angry. Tired of being mad.

I want to feel something else. I want to *be able* to feel something else. I want to let something else in.

Someone else.

That is, if that someone else wants to be let in.

I reach for my phone. I'm not ready yet to call, but I can send a text. I can manage that much. So I open a note to Chris, and I type.

I can't wait to see you tomorrow.

I hit send, and that small little action feels like the start of a big step.

Chapter Fifteen

I spend more time than usual getting ready for my Friday night date. And since I've never been one to speed-dress, that means I take a few hours, and I enjoy every single one of the minutes. Tonight's date with Chris feels like a new beginning. It feels like a real first date, but with someone I'm already sure I like. So I shave my legs, and spread the softest pomegranate lotion into my skin, thinking of how it would feel if Chris' hands were the ones on my legs. I blow out my hair, imagining his fingers twined in my hair.

I do my make-up as I listen to all my favorite songs, like *I've Got a Crush on You* and *Fly me to the Moon*, feeling that sweet possibility in the words. It's as if I'm living in the lyrics, wrapped up in the hope that they might deliver for me. I even find myself swaying to the words as I swipe on my blush.

I grab a skirt, a cute little bluish-green corduroy number, pull on my fuchsia boots, then pick a magenta-colored short sleeve sweater, near enough in color to complement the boots, far enough away so as not to be matchy-match. I make my way to my jewelry collection on my bureau. I choose a black necklace with a big black plastic heart on it and a bright pink fake gem in the middle of that. I push a trio of bracelets onto my right wrist – light pink, aqua and light blue. I switch from the lime-green purse to a basic black clutch, say good-bye to my dog, and catch a cab.

When I get out of the car, I see Chris, five feet in front of me, wearing headphones and holding an iPod. The studio he shoots promos at is near Circa Rose, so he must have walked here. Nerves slam into me. All that warm fuzziness of my alone time flies away, and now I'm faced with the does-he-or-doesn't-he-like-me dilemma. After all, he didn't text me back last night. But when he sees me, he smiles and takes the earphones out. His smile warms me.

"What are you listening to?"

"A podcast."

"On what?"

"You're going to laugh."

"So make me laugh, Chris McCormick," I say playfully as we reach Circa Rose.

"It's on how to build a car."

"You're going to build a car? Like from scratch?"

He shrugs. "I'm thinking about it," he says as he opens the door for me, then pulls out a stool for me when we reach the bar. I sit down, careful to cross my legs. My corduroy skirt isn't butt-cheek length, but it's not long either. The bartender appears. I order a grapefruit juice and vodka, Chris a beer. An image flashes through my mind – or maybe it's my senses – of the taste of beer on his lips. I can sort of taste the cold fizz, the slight chill from the drink, mixed with his breath. And I want to taste it for real. I want to tell him the contest is off. But how do I broach it especially when I don't know if he feels the same way?

He taps his iPod. "I've got podcasts on how to make your own TV, how to get your computer to go faster, how to build your own Web cam."

There's my entry. A joke to slide into the serious.

I smack my forehead. "I forgot my iCam. I forgot my computer. I've been video recording the dates, so the viewers can vote."

"Are you like the biggest dork in the world or what? What about the cat camera I fixed for you?"

The bartender returns with our drinks. Chris pays immediately before I have the chance to reach into my little black bag.

"I forgot that too."

He laughs and shakes his head, his hair falling in his eyes as he leans closer to me. I so want to reach out and touch his hair, but he never responded to my text last night, so maybe this is all just business for him. I press my palms against the bar, so I don't start running my fingers through his hair here and now.

"You could use your phone."

"I could. But I don't want to."

"You don't want to?"

"No," I say, and I am nearly paralyzed by nerves. I'm barely able to breathe any more. My chest suddenly feels constricted, as if all my fears are gripping me.

He tilts his head to the side. "Why? Am I out of the running? You don't want me to get past the first round."

"I totally want you to get past the first round."

"So then?"

There's a hopeful sound to his voice, but I can't quite form the words. I don't know how to give voice to all the feelings that are building inside me. I don't have to though because he inches his hand across the bar and loops his fingers through mine. As he clasps my hand in his, sparks race through my body, and I find myself leaning closer to him.

"I don't want to date you for the cameras," I say.

"Do you want to date me not for the cameras?" He squeezes my hand, as he holds my gaze so tight.

"Yes. I want to go out with you for you."

His eyes light up and his flirty, happy smile matches mine. "I want to go out with you for you too, McKenna."

That's all it takes for that crazy torquing feeling to fade away, and for me to move in closer and trace his top lip with my index finger. "You have really pretty lips," I say.

He laughs. "Cute blushing. Pretty lips. Are these compliments?"

"It's me. I'm a dork. I don't know what to say to someone I really like."

"So you really like me?"

"I sent you that text last night, didn't I?"

"Well, I didn't know if it was a business text, like you couldn't wait to see me for the contest, or if it was more."

"That's why you never responded?"

He nods. "Yeah, that's why I never responded. But I couldn't wait to see you too. You could throw the contest out the window right now and I would still want to date you. I would still want to play video games with you and fix your camera and have dinner with you. And I would still want to take you back to my house. And I would still want to take you out again the next day."

"You would?"

"Yes. I told you I thought you were hot the very first time I met you, and then we talked and you were so much more."

"I am?" My heart is ping ponging with happiness inside me.

"Yeah, you are. You're tough, and you're smart, and you're intensely independent, and you like music, and you're just this totally cool chick."

"So, speaking of music, you got any music on that bad boy or are you just geeking out with your DIY podcasts?"

"I have many songs. Would you like to see?"

"Yes."

"I have a whole playlist of cover songs," Chris continues. He touches the menu button and scrolls through to his playlists, tapping on the one for covers. I lean in close to read the names, and he wraps his arm around my waist. It's such a *date* gesture and

152

such an unfamiliar one to me, but as his fingertips press against my hip bone, I know I could get used to this with him. I could so get used to the feel of his hands on me, from how he touched my face when we kissed by the car last weekend, to how he played my fingers in the electronics store, and to the way he's holding me now. It borders on a possessive gesture, as if he's saying that I'm with him.

And that is what he's saying. Because right here, right now, I am with him. I shift closer, and he holds me tighter, and it's getting increasingly harder to concentrate on anything but his touch.

I try though, tapping the playlist. "*Killing Me Softly* by the Fugees. I love that. I am telling you, that is how that song was meant to be sung."

"Couldn't agree more. Same goes for *Physical* by Jane Black. So much better than Olivia Newton-John's version, don't you think?"

"Hell yeah."

"She did to that song what Aretha did to Otis Redding with *Respect*. 'That girl done stole my song,' is what he said."

I laugh, then look at his playlist again. "*Hallelujah* by Jeff Buckley. Love that version."

"It's so haunting, don't you think?" I look at him, seeing something, a passion, a spark, in those amazing green eyes of his. "I don't think there is a more beautiful song. I love it every time I hear it."

I enjoy hearing him talk about music, open up a bit about what moves him. I love that he thinks *Hallelujah* is a beautiful song, and not just because I happen to agree. I love that he loves it because that shows he has passion, he has feeling, he can be moved by a song. I love his clothes, and I love his hair, and I love his beautiful face, and his strong hands, and the way he touches, and if this keeps up there won't be enough room inside me for all of the feelings that I can barely contain. It's like a waterfall, how suddenly this rush has come over me, and I want to be close to him.

But I am so scared, and I am so good at finding ways to bat those feeling aside.

"You know what I would name my band if I were in a band? Cult of the Neon Santas. So that's what I named my wireless network."

"Bet that gets all your rock star desires out of your system. Mine would be Pizza for Breakfast."

"I love that name and having that on the menu," I say, then take a drink of my grapefruit and vodka. "You want to know why I'm not a rock star, Chris?"

"Why are you not a rock star, McKenna?"

"It's not because I can't sing. It's not because I can't hit a note if my life depended on it. And it's not because I can't play a guitar," I say, layering in a pause for effect. "It's because I can't stand being in a car for more than one hour. It would make me *crazy* having to drive all over this country from gig to shining gig."

Chris laughs, then tucks a strand of my hair back behind my ear. "You're funny, McKenna."

I'm funny. He says I'm funny. I feel like Rudolph the red-nosed reindeer when Clarice tells him he's cute. Rudolph scampers off, joyous and happy, shouting, "She thinks I'm cute! She thinks I'm cute!"

I could so fall in love with him. I could fall in love with him in a heartbeat. He brings his other hand to my waist, and pulls me in close. He's seated on the bar stool, and I'm standing as I slide into the V between his legs, his firm thighs now on either side of me. The distance between us narrows, and the temperature rises. Like this, with him so close, I can tell how much he wants me. As much as I want him. I am turned on beyond belief, my skin is so hot, and

154

my body is aching all over with the need to be touched, and he knows it. And just like that, the mood between us here at Circa Rose shifts. It's no longer flirty, or chatty, or get to know you. We're no longer a guy and girl confessing to crushes and likes. As he plays with the waistband of my skirt, his hand dipping inside, stroking the bare skin of my hips just above my panties, we are a man and a woman who want to get the hell out of here. The air between us is electric, like the moments before a summer storm.

"We don't need to shoot that promo anymore, do we?" he asks, and his voice is different now too. It's smoky and low, and as he brings me in closer, I can tell he's gone to the same place I've gone to. Desire. And then the hope that we can take this contact to another level.

"I was really hoping to see your fancy studio though," I tease.

"It has a nice couch."

"We could do a lot on a couch."

"It's ten blocks away."

"That's far," I say, and I'm keenly aware of how my voice has become a ragged whisper. He has to know what I want right now. *Him*. His green eyes are dark, shadowed with lust and staring intensely into mine. He's waiting for me to say more. "But I think I really want to see that couch."

"Good, because I would really fucking love to make out with you properly right now."

There is no option to do anything else. There is no way I will go anywhere right now, but to this studio that's ten blocks away. I cannot conceive of doing anything else in this moment but being alone with Chris. He takes my hand, gripping it tight, and guides me to the front of the bar, then the sidewalk. In seconds flat, he's hailed a cab.

"That's no small feat to hail a cab quickly in San Francisco," I say as we slide inside.

"It's part of the guy code. All the cabbies in the world have this special alert to show up quickly when a guy really needs to be alone with his woman."

I start to laugh, but my laughter is smothered by his lips on mine, and soon I'm grabbing at his shirt, and he's cupping the back of my head, and we are a fevered picture of two people who can't get enough of each other. Then the cab stops, Chris pays, and we're at the door of a three-story brick office building that's dark except for one light in the lobby.

"This isn't where you shoot your show, right?" I ask as he fishes in his pocket for the keys. My hands toy with the waistband of his jeans.

He shakes his head. "No. The network's over in the Dogpatch, near the other TV shows shot in town. This is just a tiny little studio for pick-ups, promos, quickies." He winks at the last word as he unlocks the door and holds it open for me.

Using his cell phone for light, we walk quickly up a darkened stairwell, then Chris pushes open a heavy door that leads into a short hallway. He flicks on the light switch. At the end of the hall is a door with a white lacquered sign that reads *Fish Out of Water Studios*.

"Clever name," I remark.

"Like a band name. Or wireless network name," he replies as he opens that door and turns on the light. The space is split in two by a glass window. The studio itself is beyond the glass and it's tiny – but even in the dark I can tell it has a green screen on one wall, a camera, and lights. We're in the waiting area and there's a desk with a desk calendar, a computer and pens, and the aforementioned couch.

But we don't make it to the couch. Instead, I back up quickly against the wall and pull him close to me, my fingers tapping out a staccato rhythm on his belly. "We can't go all the way," I say.

"That's fine."

"I'm just not ready."

"It's okay. We don't have to. Whatever you want to do is fine, but I just want you to know this. The real reason I agreed to do your contest wasn't to promote my show. I couldn't care less. I did it because I wanted to be in the running. I want to be the only one in the running. I want you."

"You are. The only one," I say, and I'm nearly breathless as he grazes my arm lazily with the tips of his fingers.

"Good. Because I'm not even thinking about the contest anymore."

"You're not?"

"Not in the least."

"What are you thinking about?"

He looks me straight in the eyes, disarmingly, holding my gaze. "What I want to do to you now."

I can feel the soft little hairs on my arms standing on end. "What do you want to do?"

He lays a hand on my bare leg. His hand is warm, his skin is soft, he feels good. "This." His voice is strong. He's not playing around. He's just a man speaking his mind.

My back is to the wall, and he's looking at me, and his hand is on my thigh, tracing the edge of my short, short skirt. He raises an eyebrow as his fingers cross over, slipping inside my skirt. It feels so good, I want to cry. I haven't been touched in so long, I nearly forgot what it can do to a girl. My whole body feels alive, as if every part of me is reaching for him, longing for him.

"It feels so good," I tell him.

"*You* feel so good. Don't take this the wrong way. Don't take this to mean I don't like you, because I do. But I have totally wanted to get in your pants since the day I met you."

"Yeah. I think I can take that the right way."

He moves his hand higher, inching so close to my inner thighs, where I'm throbbing for him. There's no other way to describe it. Because I am simply dying to be touched by him. He makes me feel so wanted, so desired, and so cared for, it's intoxicating. I'm so turned on by him, pulsing with all these feelings that collide inside of me at once – the pure physical desire, but then the way my heart feels unfrozen with him, un-angry. The way it feels a crazy kind of joy that I could live off, that could feed me. His touch could too. His hands are strong and insistent, but gentle in their own way too as he traces the outside of my panties. I am racing right now, and my panties are damp, and he smiles a wicked little grin as he touches them for the first time.

"That's fucking awesome," he whispers in my ear. "I love how wet you are."

"Well, the cat's out of the bag, Chris. You turn me on something crazy."

"Good. Because I've been thinking about doing this. I've thought about this when I'm in the shower," he says, and I might as well rocket into another world of pleasure. He just told me he's gotten off to me. I didn't think it were possible to feel any more heat, but I am aflame.

"You think about me in the shower?"

"I have had many, many thoughts about you. I have touched you in so many ways already," he says, his voice, low and dirty in my ear. The ache between my legs intensifies, and I am longing for him to touch me, to know what he's done to me.

"Like how?"

"I've tasted you. I've touched you. I've been inside you, and now I want to feel you for real."

I might swoon with desire, but there's no time to do anything but gasp, as he slides his hand inside my panties, and an involuntary moan escapes me at the first touch. Oh my god. This is what it feels like without batteries. This is what it feels like with someone else's hands. This is what it's like when someone wants to touch you as much as you want to be touched.

"Chris," I say in a low voice.

"Yes?"

"I've thought about you too. I've thought about you touching me."

"You have?"

I nod. "Yes. Before our first Guitar Hero lesson. You made me come," I say, and it's a hushed and hot confession. The look in his eyes is one of lust and heat, and it's about the sexiest a man has ever been.

"How? How did I do it?" His voice is rough, full of unchained desire.

"You went down on me," I whisper.

He nearly growls at my admission. "And you tasted spectacular. Because I was making you come the night before too. By licking you, by going down on you and you were grabbing my face and pulling me closer," he says in a husky voice. "God, I am dying to make you come right now."

His words turn me molten, and I close my eyes, and breathe out hard as he grazes me with those strong fingers. I shift my stance, so my legs are open wider, while my pink boots are pressed firmly on the ground. He moves in closer, his fingers gliding across me as he presses his body against me. I grab hold of his hip with one hand and angle him so I can feel how hard he is against my thigh, as his fingers slide across my silky wetness.

I breathe out harder, whimpers and sighs falling from my lips with abandon. I can't pretend any more. I can't fake it anymore. I can't be cool, cold, business McKenna with Chris. Not like this. Not as the world tilts away, and I am reduced to one exquisite point in my body, as I arch into his hand.

He doesn't even need to slide a finger inside me. There's no need, because he's so good, and I'm so ready, that the way he works me in a perfect rhythm, up and down, and then there, right there, where I want him, where I start singing his praises over and over, is all I need, all I want, all I know right now. I am gasping and panting and my hips rock into his hand.

"You are so hot, McKenna. You are so ridiculously hot all the time, but especially right now," he whispers to me. "The way your lips are parted, and your eyes are closed, and your body moves against me. I've thought about doing this in your friend's car the other night. You have no idea how much I wanted to touch you."

I feel so vulnerable, as if this moment is a line in the sand, and it is. Because I'm going to come any second, I am going to come with this man, this former candidate, this possible boyfriend, this person who has entered my life in the most random of ways, and who I could never resist, and I am only going to want him more and more and again and again.

"Chris," I say, my voice breaking. "You say those things, and you're going to make me come soon."

"I want to bring you there, babe. I want to make you come hard for me and say my name," he says, and as I feel myself building to that delirious point of no return, I grab his hair, his soft surfer boy hair that falls through my fingers, so unbelievably soft.

I hold onto him as I squeeze my eyes shut from the sensations that topple through me. I am not quiet, I do not muffle my sounds, I don't hold anything back, as I say Chris' name over and over and over as the first orgasm I haven't given myself in ages crashes through me. And moments later, even as the blissful aftershocks radiate, all I can think is I wasn't waiting for him, I had no way of knowing he'd come into my life, but he was worth waiting for.

"I'm so glad you wore a skirt tonight. Can you always wear short skirts, so I can get you off in studios, or cabs, or wherever we are?"

I finally open my eyes and I'm sure I'm glowing. "Who would have thought that you could be such a cute blusher and such a dirty talker?"

He smiles with pride. "You bring it out in me. Both."

Now, I may not have had sex in a year, but I'm not the Virgin Mary, and I'm not a prude, and I've never been one to leave a guy hanging, so I tell him I want to return the favor.

"I want to touch you."

"Right here?"

"Well, you did me right here in your quickie promo studio. Shouldn't you get the same star treatment?"

"I could argue with you, but somehow I think it would be pointless."

"Do you want to argue with me?"

He shakes his head as I press my palm against him through his jeans. He moans, and the sound of his pleasure make me happy, ridiculously happy. I like Chris so much, I want him to feel good. I want to bring him to that same place he brought me, and some things are like riding a bike.

"Have you pictured this too?"

"Yes." His voice is low, and his eyes sear into me with his one-word answer.

"You've imagined me touching you?"

"Yes." I can hear the need in his voice.

"And more?"

He nods, his eyes never leaving mine, everything in his intense gaze, his voice, the strain of his erection against my hand, telling me what I do to him. How much he wants me. His desire turns me magnetic, and I want to crash into him. Because I want to be wanted. I want to be wanted like this. By him.

"You've thought about me going down on you?"

He breathes out hard. "I've thought about your lips on me," he says, as he runs a fingertip against my top lip. "These lips of yours…"

I take his finger into my mouth, and he curses, his eyes nearly rolling back into his head as I tease him.

"*McKenna*," he says, hungrily.

"Yes, Chris?" I ask, as if I don't know the answer.

He brings my face close to his, his forehead against mine, and he whispers hoarsely. "Please touch me."

I kneel down, unzip his jeans, lower his boxer briefs, and then enjoy the view. He's so hard, and if I were the kind of girl who liked to kiss and tell I could totally compete with my sister right now, but I no longer want to kiss and tell. I no longer want the world to know what I'm up to. I only want him. I look up at him.

"I like what I see," I tell him, a glint in my eyes.

"Good."

Then I take him in my mouth, and he groans, and the noises he makes are music to my ears. I love the way he responds to my lips, to my tongue, to my mouth on him. I love how he says my name as I take him in further, and wrap a hand around him too, and it sends me into another stratosphere of pleasure, as if I could come again without even being touched, as his hands thread through my hair, grappling to hold on, and he says my name in this sexy, heady voice as he comes.

Soon, we straighten ourselves out, and head down the hall, separating briefly for bathroom breaks. Then I rejoin him and we leave the building together, holding hands. Out on the street, the night air is chilly. I shiver, and he pulls me in close as we walk.

"I like dating for real. Are you free all weekend?"

"Yes."

"Tomorrow, I want to take you to a karaoke bar in Japan Town that you'll love."

"I love karaoke."

"But there's one condition."

"Okay," I say tentatively.

"You need to call the contest off."

I smile. "Obviously. It's so over, it's beyond over. I mean, I was totally going to tell you that. I was planning on saying that all night, but I was having such a good time dating you."

"And other things."

"And other things," I add.

"Good. Because I'm not sharing you, and I'm not competing with anyone, and I definitely don't want you dating anyone besides me."

I part my lips and am about to say "I'm yours." But I can't quite go there yet. Instead, I nod, and say "The next Fashion Hound will be the announcement that I don't need or want a Trophy Husband anymore."

"Can I be your trophy boyfriend?"

Boyfriend. There's that sweet, magical word again. There's the word that has mattered, the word that I wanted, but I let another word get in the way. Because the truth is I know what I want. I've known since way back when I first went trolling for a Trophy Husband on Craigslist. I knew then I wanted a boyfriend, not a husband. Now, I just know who I want that boyfriend to be.

I am all grins, and I'm sure that this is what happy looks like as I say yes.

Chapter Sixteen

I ignore the comments on my Web site asking where's the footage of my Friday night date with Chris. My viewers all know the date was last night. They were expecting to see how it went. I want to jump for joy in my next video and tell them it went fabulously.

But there will be time for that. For now, I am working on my concession speech. I'm lounging on a deck chair, sunglasses on and Ms. Pac-Man at my feet panting from our tennis ball in the waves session a few minutes ago. I'm trying to find the right mix of humor and contrition. Do I tell my viewers *"Sorry, Contest over?"* Or do I give a lengthy explanation about my change of heart?

I stare at a blank page on my laptop. I'm not usually at a loss for words. I'm pretty damn fast at whipping out my blogs and assessing outfits with the 1-2-3 snappiness of a sassy cable show host. But when it comes to penning my own truths about the heart? Well, the keyboard might as well be written in a foreign language.

When my phone rings, I am thrilled for the distraction.

Then I see Todd's name flash across the screen. I would like to ignore him. I really would. But I don't trust him, and that's the problem. Untrustworthy people, by their nature, demand attention because they are loose cannons.

"What's up?" I say in a resigned voice.

Ms. Pac-Man tilts her ears as if she's listening. I like to think she's protecting me from him. But then, I don't think anyone, even if my dog, could have protected me from the damage Todd inflicted with one shot.

"How are you, McKenna?"

"Fine. But you're not calling to chat, so what is it?"

"I was just thinking," he begins, and then inserts that pregnant pause that marks all his conversations.

I roll my eyes, even though he can't see me. "What were you thinking?"

"I was thinking about how I helped you start The Fashion Hound. Remember?"

When I first came up with the idea for my show, I shared it with Todd and he encouraged me to go for it. He also set up my Web site, bought the domain, and installed my first blog template. He worked in tech PR and he knew his way around the tools of the Internet. I could have done that all myself, but he wanted to help, so I could focus on the writing, and the fashions and finding a talented videographer.

My chest tightens with worry. "Yes. What are you getting at?"

Then I hear a baby cry.

"The baby just woke up from her nap. I'll call you later."

He doesn't call back, and I hate the way I carry my phone around the rest of the afternoon, even as I get ready for another date with Chris. But there was something in Todd's voice that made me uneasy, and now I have a knot of worry pooling low in my gut. I wish he could leave me alone, so I do a few yoga moves, stretch my neck from side to side, and tell myself everything will be all right.

Then I head to the karaoke bar.

Because tonight, I am with Chris, and I want to only be with Chris. I don't even want the ghost of my ex infecting this night.

I listen to him adorably bungling his way through Foreigner's *Jukebox Hero* in a fetchingly off-key singing voice. He's wearing jeans and a brown tee-shirt. The design on his shirt is of two ultra-stylized dinosaurs in orange silhouette sparring with each other. I love his taste in clothes.

He sings from the low stage at Gomez Hawks Karaoke Bar, deep in the heart of Japan Town, tucked in a dark corner of the second floor of a mall that's stuffed with Japanese bookstores, crepe dealers, sushi bars and other assorted Tokyo-flavored shops. Chris finishes his number, does a quick little bow, and bounds off stage to join me at the bar.

"Very nice, Mr. McCormick," I say, nodding approvingly.

He shrugs. "I have a horrible singing voice."

"I thought it was cute."

"Cute blushing, cute singing, pretty lips."

"Hey! I told you this is all new to me. I'm working on my lines for you."

"Don't use lines on me," he teases.

"So isn't your sister a Broadway singer or something?"

"Yeah, but that doesn't mean the rest of us have her talent. Besides, she has no mechanical aptitude and there's where I have all my skills." He cracks his knuckles in a playful way as if to demonstrate his skill with his hands. He does have skill with his hands.

"So when does her show open? *Crash the Moon*, right?"

"Two more months, I think. I'm going to see it opening night."

"Well, of course. You have to."

"I am going to be the one cheering the loudest and longest. Well, all of us will be." Then he leans his shoulder against mine. "You should come with me."

"To New York?"

"No. To Istanbul. Yes, New York. That's where the show is."

My heart skips a few beats. He's making plans with me two months from now. "I would love to."

"Now why don't you do some cute singing yourself then." He gestures to the stage.

"I will," I say, as I toss the list of karaoke songs aside.

Gomez Hawks is a tiny bar, the whole place no bigger than my living room. But it's low-lit and serves terrific mixed drinks and boasts the biggest and best selection of songs in the city, a list about the size of two New York City phone books put together. That's why Gomez Hawks is popular and that's why Chris made a reservation tonight. All the tables are full, all the stools are taken. I begin with a few astronomically off-key "whoa, whoa, whoas" of my own before I launch into the opening lines about Tommy's work on the docks in Bon Jovi's anthemic song and karaoke standard.

Immediately, everyone in the bar is singing along, some by memory, others by following the TV screen with the flashing lyrics from the song. Three minutes later, we're as loud as loud can be finishing the final words of *Livin' on a Prayer* in unison. The crowd cheers their approval, despite my lack of harmony, melody and anything in between. But it's karaoke. You're not supposed to sing well.

I rejoin Chris at the bar. "How do you think this place got its name?"

"I have a hunch the proprietor was racking his brains for a catchy name, drove past a street named Gomez and then a high school with a football team called the Hawks and mashed them together."

I laugh. "Is that for real? Do you know that?"

"No, but it sounded plausible, didn't it?"

167

"Totally. You know what would be even more fun? If karaoke was a game and you could earn points for songs and hitting the notes or something. Even though I'd suck, I'd still play."

"Of course you would. You're even more of a gamer than I am."

"Not anymore. I'm all ready to call the whole thing off on Monday."

"Good. Because I can't stand the thought of anyone else thinking they have a shot for you. I want you all to myself." He loops his hand around my waist and pulls me in for a kiss. It's a protective kiss, and it feels a bit like ownership. Like he's claiming me. I don't mind being his. I don't mind at all.

"Did you kiss any of the other guys when you were dating the candidates?"

"No. Only you. I told you. I wanted to jump you the second I saw you. Oh wait. That's what you told me," I say and I grin.

"I did. I still do."

"I want that too," I say in a low voice.

"Yeah?"

"I do. Soon."

"Like I told you, I'll wait for whenever you're ready."

"But we can do other things…"

He raises an eyebrow. "There are plenty of other things I want to do to you."

"Like what?"

He's about to answer when I hear a strain of familiar notes playing from the karaoke machine. I turn to the stage. There's an older man on stage, graying, and with a paunch. He wears glasses and high-waisted pants, but he has a huge smile on his face. He's looking at a woman, seated at a table near the front. She has curly gray hair and lines around her eyes. I glance at their hands. Rings on their fingers.

Then he brings the microphone to his mouth and begins doing his best imitation of The King as he sings about fools rushing in. The lyrics swoop into me, and even though he doesn't sing like Elvis, not even close, the look on his face as he sings to his wife, only to his wife, about how he can't help falling in love, slays me like it does every time.

I remember one of the last times I heard this song. Driving to The Best Doughnut Shop in the City. The day I fell apart and hid in a bathroom stall. I think back to this afternoon, to the phone call, to the way Todd needles me. I can let him get under my skin, or I can let go of my anger.

Is there really a choice?

I have to choose to let go of my ex. Because now I'm here, and I'm not just longing for the feelings in this song.

I'm feeling them.

I lean into Chris, my back against his chest, and he wraps his arms around my waist, pulling me close. We sway slightly, almost imperceptibly, as the man sings. When he reaches the words "take my hand" the man does just that and his wife holds her hand out to him. They're not touching. They're many feet apart. Still, it's the most romantic thing I've ever seen.

Until Chris takes my hand. Laces his fingers through mine. Squeezes.

When the music fades, he turns me around so he's looking at me. "I know you're not ready for more, but how would you feel about coming back to my place so I can do all those other things I've thought about doing?"

"You mean play Qbert?" I tease.

"If that's what you want to call it."

* * *

Chris lives in a cream-colored Victorian building, with muted green trim on the windows and the door. His home is above an antique shop and right next door to Barney's Burger Joint, which received the "Best Burgers in San Francisco in 2007" honor from a local paper.

He unlocks the main door, and we walk up two flights of stairs. As we round the stairwell, his hands are on my waist, and he's telling me all the things he wants to do to me.

"You know it's not going to take me long when you talk like that."

"Good. Then we can go again."

He opens the door to his place and it's spacious. The living room is wide and stretches the whole length of the building it seems. I spot a few arcade games off in the corner, including Qbert, and I pretend I'm a zombie, drawn to it. Chris puts both hands on my shoulders and steers me away. "We'll get to those soon enough," he teases.

I look around the rest of the living room. A high-definition TV screen is mounted on the off-white wall, flanked by several gaming consoles. Chris told me once he spends close to fifteen hours a week playing games. "Sounds glamorous and it is when the games are good," he'd said. "But sometimes, it's drudgery."

There's a huge U-shaped couch against the opposite wall, in some sort of indistinct gray color. But it looks cushy and well-worn and is stuffed with brown and burnished gold pillows in the corners. His kitchen is modern and sleek with stainless steel appliances, but it doesn't scream "bachelor cool." There's an antique-y table against the wall, with curvy legs, while a pale yellow tea kettle sits in the middle of the stove.

Chris then gestures vaguely to the other room. "The boudoir. But you can't see that tonight," he says playfully. I land on the side of good taste and opt not to peer into his bedroom, but I notice out of the corner of my eye he has a king-size bed with a beige cover, white walls, and blond book shelves beside the headboard.

"So there you go," he says, leaning against the wall in his hallway, hooking his thumbs through the belt loops on his jeans. I can't help myself. My eyes drift down to the bulge in his pants. How am I going to refrain from taking his clothes off and wrapping my legs around him? But I know once we go there, I'll be gone for him. I'll be more over the moon than I already am. Once he's inside me, there will be no turning back.

I want to, I'm almost there, but yet the possibility of being shattered in a million pieces again prevents me from taking that step. So I turn away and walk to Qbert. I run a hand across the control panel, feeling the joystick against my palm. I trace my fingers across the name in its big, balloon-y print. Then I peek at the side of the machine. The entire side panel is a bright bold yellow with an illustration of Qbert cursing as he nears the edge of the pyramid. I return to the screen and lay my cheek against it.

"You sure you don't want me to leave you alone with it?"

"I have other plans," I say, but then I'm distracted when I notice the Galaga machine to the right, then a Donkey Kong.

"My God, you have your own arcade."

He joins me by the games. "Would you be impressed if I told you I built them all myself?"

My eyes open wide. I can't believe what he is saying. My brain is about to pop. "You built an arcade game?"

"You make it sound like I made a time machine out of a Delorean. It wasn't that hard."

"Wasn't that hard?" I parrot back. "How do you *make* an arcade game?"

"I dusted off an old computer, found some source code from this non-profit development project that preserves old arcade games, tweaked it up a bit and then built the cabinet."

"This is amazing. You have some serious *skills*," I say.

"And you haven't even seen me surf. I can ride some serious waves."

"You can ride this wave," I say suggestively. "You can *make* this wave." I hop up on the Qbert, and sit on the console, my legs dangling in front of the machine. I glance down at my skirt, and he gets the hint.

"You on my Qbert machine might possibly blow my mind. But I'm willing to try."

He runs his hands through my hair and kisses me hard, as if he needs to kiss me first for foreplay or something. But even a whisper of a kiss from him is all I need. Besides, I've been ready for this since the karaoke bar.

He moves to my neck, kissing me there, then pulls off my shirt, cupping my breasts with my bra on. He unhooks it in seconds flat, and his tongue flicks over a nipple, then the other one and I lean my head back and say his name, and that sound moves him further down my body, as he kisses my belly, then pushes up my skirt. He's gentle as he lifts my butt and wiggles off my underwear, careful to make sure I don't bonk the joystick. Then he bends lower, kissing the inside of my thighs, softly, trailing his tongue from my knee all the way up, then darting over to the other leg.

I am electric and fiery from every touch of him, and I am dying to feel his mouth on me. I want to pull him between my thighs so he can taste me, lick me, press his lips against my warm wetness, and do all the things he said he wants to do.

"Chris," I moan, since he's teasing me, toying with me, making me want him more.

He nibbles lightly on my thigh, as his strong hands spread my legs wider. I accidentally bump the start button, and even though he hasn't put a quarter in the game, the theme music from Qbert begins. I laugh, and so does he, but then my laugh turns into a long, low moan at the first flick of his tongue on me. He makes this sound too, like a rumble, as he tastes how ready I am for him. It's like an altered state I've entered, and my whole body is crackling with heat. He is magnificent, his tongue divine as he traces delirious lines up and down my center that make me whimper.

My noises drive him, and each sound that tumbles from my lips makes him hungrier for me, and we become this perfect feedback loop of wanting, and giving, and taking as I grow wetter and hotter with every single touch. I am in heaven with him, I am in a white-hot dream. I grip the edge of the game console as he consumes me with his mouth, his tongue, his lips.

His mouth was tailor-made for me. He goes down on me like he's kissing me and devouring me at the same time, somehow both soft and hungry in the fevered slide of his delicious lips against my very core, driving me wild.

Then his hands slink under my thighs and he lifts my legs onto his shoulders, draping them over his back. I feel so completely vulnerable with him, as if I am giving myself to him completely, but I'm not scared anymore, because he wants what I have to give. He wants me, all of me, only me, and that's why I'm nearly panting as I say his name, and tell him how good it feels, because it does, it feels good, it feels great, it feels like everything is happening for the first time, and the best time, and that it won't be the last time. It'll be the start of something amazing with him.

Then he brings me there, and he shatters me with an orgasm that's as endless as it is intense. I let go of the side of the game, and I grab his hair, his ridiculously soft hair that slides through my fingers, and I hold onto him as I come hard, with the kind of soundtrack that drives neighbors jealous.

Soon, when I can form words again, and when he's standing and looking at me with those dreamy eyes that say everything I want, I kiss him, tasting myself on him, tasting what he just did to me. He loops his arms around me, and I lean my head on his chest. "That was out of this world. You know how to go down on a girl."

He kisses my forehead. "I know how to go down on you because I want you. Because I can't get enough of you."

"You are the best boyfriend I've ever had."

"Good. Let's keep it that way."

Those words feel a bit like a promise, and that promise feels a bit like falling in love.

Chapter Seventeen

The afterglow lasts through Sunday as I spend the afternoon strolling through my favorite boutiques in Noe Valley with Hayden and Erin.

Erin prowls through a rack, then shows me an adorable cream sweater with little pearl buttons and tiny baby blue embroidered birds. "It's so kitschy cute I almost can't stand it," she says as she holds it against my chest. She looks at Hayden. "She should wear this on her next date, don't you think?"

"Definitely." Hayden nods her approval. Then taps her lips with her index finger, and furrows her brow. "But for what guy?"

"JP?" Erin asks, then shakes her head. "Nope. Chris. Wear this on your next date with Chris."

Erin thrusts the sweater into my hands, and I know this is the moment. This is when I should tell them. I should let them know that the dates with Chris are real and that the sweater could truly be for me to wear with him. That the contest is over and I have a boyfriend rather than a husband. And I like it that way. No, I *love* it that way.

"So, um," I start to say, then my voice becomes vapor.

And it hits me why. It's not that I'm afraid of disappointing them. They care about me more than a contest. They'll forgive me for lying about his age. They'll probably even laugh about it, and about my worries over breaking an oath that was all fun and games. What they've truly wanted for me all along is to heal from heartbreak. That's precisely what makes me clam up. Fear of heartbreak. Of getting hurt. Of being broken. Because there's a part of me that knows as soon as I give voice to what's happening with Chris, then I may very well have to tell them someday about it ending. It's as if I am trying to hold it in my hands, like a fragile glass globe and keep it safe until it's immune from heartache, until it's safe from the breaking.

So for now I stay quiet, keeping the bloom of falling for Chris to myself through the evening, as I walk my dog, and read a text from my boyfriend telling me that Qbert misses me, and it's almost enough for me to drop everything and invite him over. But the next time I see him I know I'll want him in every way, and I won't let myself go there until I've come clean. So I resist, telling him instead that I've never enjoyed a game of Qbert more.

Then I reach for my laptop, write out a script for tomorrow's show, going with the simplest admission of all. "Thanks for your support. I'm pleased to let you know that I found someone who makes me ridiculously happy, and because of that the contest is over. It wouldn't be fair to him, you, me or anyone else to keep going because this guy has already won. He's won my heart."

I exhale.

I've written it down. I've given voice to my feelings. I'll be putting it out there. I can do this. I can step forward into the great unknown of a new love. Tomorrow, I'll call Hayden, Erin and Julia right after my shoot and before the video goes live.

I close the computer, slide under the covers, and scratch Ms. Pac-Man's ears just the way she likes.

"You're a good girl."

* * *

The next morning as I finish my makeup, Todd's name flashes across my phone. My stomach tightens, but I answer it anyway. He's holding something over me, and I need to know what it is.

"So about the sale of your blog to Fashion Nation," he begins, picking up our truncated call where we left off. "I hate to do this, McKenna. I really hate to do this. But I feel a little bit, what's the word? Shafted. A little bit shafted. Left out with the sale."

I must get my hearing checked. I'm sure he didn't just say that. "You feel shafted? Well, isn't that just the pot calling the kettle black."

He ignores me. "I'm only talking about what's fair. You made a pretty penny on that sale, and you surely deserve most of it." I grit my teeth as he repeats the words, "Most of it."

"I deserve all of it."

"Well, I'm not so sure about that. And I've been talking to some folks who think it's a little unfair that I didn't receive any of the buyout money. After all, I did play an instrumental role in the intellectual property of The Fashion Hound. If not for me, you would probably never even have a blog."

He is gasoline and I am a flame. "Let me guess. You're not making as much money as your new wife wants to support your family. So you're looking to dip your fingers in my bank account?"

He scoffs. "No. No. No. I want what's fair. This isn't about money. This is about equality. That's something that matters a lot to you, isn't it? You're all about equality. You're going after equal treatment in your show with your little project. I want equal treatment in the sale."

I am fuming, twin streams of red fury pour out of my ears, as I slam my mascara tube on the sink, only one eye done. I am a teapot about to boil over, a geyser about to blow. "I would rather wear baggy jeans and shapeless shirts for the rest of my life than ever give you a cent of what you don't deserve."

I stab my manicured nail on the end button and drop my phone on the chair. Then I race downstairs, and bang on Hayden's door, hoping to hell she hasn't left yet for work.

She answers, dressed sharply in her lawyer suit, a cup of coffee in one hand.

"Greg," I say, through clenched teeth. "I need to talk to Greg."

"He's leaving for work in a few, but come in."

I walk inside, not caring that mascara has made it onto only one set of eyelashes, and that my face must look oddly asymmetrical as I collapse at the kitchen table and lay out my newest dilemma for Hayden's business attorney husband. He nods thoughtfully, listening carefully as I recount every detail of Todd's request.

"Please tell me he doesn't have a leg to stand on," I say, and I'm not just begging, I'm pleading.

Greg sighs. "I'll help you through this. You know I will. But he has a case."

"It never ends with him."

Hayden sighs, as she puts a hand on my shoulder. She says nothing. There is nothing to say. Because Todd will stop at nothing to find new ways to rip me.

I return to my house and punch the Xbox on-button. I fire up Guitar Hero this time and plow through a few songs on medium, releasing my fury on the guitar and then taking down Slash in three tries in an epic guitar battle on the medium level.

But I still want to kick the screen, or the console, or a brick wall, so when my phone rings again, I answer it angrily before I even see who's calling.

"What. Is. It. Now?"

"Hi, I'm looking for McKenna Bell," the man's voice says, unperturbed. He's not Todd, so I dial down my anger.

"This is McKenna."

"Hello! This is Tristan Quinn. I'm a producer with *Helen* in the city and I wanted to see if you are available to come on the show today."

"Me?"

"Yes, you. *The Fashion Hound*," he coos, saying my name with a faux-sinister accent, like I'm a campy sixties superhero.

"For what?"

Helen is a national daytime talk show that's been on the air for several years. Helen is Helen Weathers, a former actress and comedian. Her show is topical, she interviews celebrities and politicians, brings popular musicians on stage to perform, and banters with the audience and guests.

"Well," Tristan purrs into the phone, "Helen just adores your video blog and wants to talk to you about what makes a good Trophy Husband."

"Oh, that's very sweet. But I'm no longer in the market for a –"

"–Helen has been a fan of your blog for some time now," Tristan gushes. He lowers his voice. "You know, she's an alpha female too."

I laugh. "I know, but–"

"And she just LOVES the idea of a Trophy Husband so she wants you on the show to talk about traits and qualities that make for a good Trophy Husband. You're the leading expert on them, she says."

"I'm the leading expert on Trophy Husbands? Wow, I didn't know the world needed one."

"Oh, I just have to tell you, I think this idea is so fabulous. I mean, men have been doing this for years. Why not women?"

"That was my thought initially, but I've sort of had a change of–"

"– So, how about today? We're over in the Dogpatch, and you're local, so maybe you can just motor on over and chat with

Helen. We tape at eleven and the segment will run this afternoon. And you can talk about how to evaluate a Trophy Husband. How to assess a Trophy Husband. Like he's a bottle of wine, a new car, a mink coat, not that I'd ever wear fur, obviously."

"Uh…"

You see, I want to tell him, I'm retiring from Trophy Husband hunting. I'm hanging up my hat. I don't want a trophy, I don't want a boy toy, thank you very much. I have a boyfriend, a delicious boyfriend, who went down on me on his Qbert machine, who wrapped his arms around me and practically sang my favorite song to me, who told me he wanted to go out with me from the first day he met me. A boyfriend who doesn't want anyone else to have me.

But Tristan's merely asking me on the show as an expert, right? He's not asking me to talk about my quest. He wants to know how to appraise boy toys. I can do that. I can help other women who'll come after me. I'll just postpone today's blog til the afternoon, and I'll go get ready for Helen's show now.

Besides, I still have fight in me. I haven't gone soft. I won't let a little peaceful easy feeling with Chris make me forget there's still a battle with my ex, and I'm not through getting even.

"I'd love to be on the show."

Chapter Eighteen

A town car arrives at my house an hour later, after I've touched up my makeup and picked out a new outfit, a perfect one for TV.

I spend the next thirty minutes on the drive pecking away at my phone, trying to whittle through the mess of email and Facebook and Web messages that have accumulated this morning. Viewers are still following the contest and want to know what's going on and why there's no report today. It's going to have to suck when I pull the plug this afternoon. But they'll be cool with it, right? I've always had a good relationship with my viewers. Everything will work out fine, everything will work out fine, everything will work out fine...

Then I see a text from Chris. *Hey, where's your video? Can't wait to see it...*

My stomach plummets. He's been waiting for my blog. There's probably a part of it that must feel like closure to him, like the final end of one relationship – my relationship with a contest – and the start of a new one. With him.

But that finality won't come until later.

I hit his number, exhaling as I wait. I feel like a heel as he answers.

"Hey."

"Hey."

There's an awkward pause and I'm sure he can read my mind and know that I haven't pulled the plug yet. "So, what are you up to?"

"I'm about to be on Helen's show," I say, and then I explain how it's my last hurrah, and then I'll bow out gracefully.

He doesn't say anything. The silence stretches through several blocks.

"Chris?"

"I'm here."

"Are you mad at me?"

He pauses and sighs, and in that sigh I hear the resignation and the frustration. "No. I just was hoping this would be over. I was hoping after this weekend that I'd have you to myself."

"But you do," I say and I wish I could hide the desperation I suddenly hear in my voice. "You do have me."

"Yeah, maybe it seems that way to you. But to me, it still feels like you're involved with some kind of crazy pursuit. With some kind of revenge thing you have going on. And hey, look. I respect the need for closure. I'm totally fine if you need more time or whatever to deal with stuff," he says and lets his voice trail off.

Stuff. Like my ex. Like all the baggage I bring. Have I not fully dealt with it? Yet, that's why I started this contest in the first place, right? Because I wanted closure with Todd. But how much more closed can our relationship be?

I sigh and try to explain. "I just want to make a point. That's all. I want to prove that women can do what men can do."

"I know, McKenna. I know," he says in a soft voice, but one tinged with resignation. "I know this is a point that's important. And what I'm saying is when this point is no longer important to you, that's when you should call me again. Goodbye."

Then he hangs up, and I am surrounded by an all-too familiar feeling of being left. Of being alone. I clench my jaw because now

I'm mad at Chris, and besides, if I don't call upon these seemingly endless stores of anger in me, I'll probably break down and cry.

And I don't want to ruin my mascara before I go on TV to make a point.

* * *

The car pulls up to Helen's studios and the chauffeur opens my door. I thank him, then reach for my pirate girl bag, keeping my chin up and my focus on. The security guard buzzes me in. I show my ID at the desk and sign the guest register.

A tall, handsome and immaculately dressed man in pressed khaki pants and a pink polo shirt greets me. His hair is light brown and his face is full of freckles.

He reaches a hand out to shake mine briskly. "McKenna Bell, I'm Tristan Quinn. So glad you could be here." He holds a clipboard in one hand and gestures with the other to the hall. I walk alongside him down an air-conditioned hallway. Photos in blond wood frames line the walls every few feet. Each one features Helen with a different guest. Singers, actors, even other Web show hosts.

I wonder if their stomachs were tied in knots before they taped as well.

* * *

I can hear Helen chattering with the audience from my backstage post. Tristan is positioned next to me. He grips his clipboard tightly. He wields that thing like a weapon, ready to brandish it at any moment. He's methodical, organized. He points to the stage and places his hand over his ear, his gesture to make sure I'm listening.

"I'm really excited about our final guest. Her name is McKenna Bell, The Fashion Hound, but you probably know her better as a woman on a mission." Tristan taps me on the shoulder, holds up his hand and begins counting down with his fingers. "Her video blog with fashion tips is a huge hit, and it's taken off like crazy in the last month since she started her own sort of reality competition online. She's looking to land a Trophy Husband. Let's say hello to McKenna Bell."

As Tristan points to the stage I walk out, the bright lights on me, a smattering of applause from the audience. Helen shakes my hand and we sit down on her white couch as the cameras keep rolling. She's wearing white slacks and sneakers, a long-sleeve button-down and a black sweater vest. I'm wearing my favorite poodle skirt, Mary Janes, and an emerald green fitted tee-shirt with my silver heart necklace. I ignore the fact that my shirt is the color of Chris' eyes.

"First of all, love the shoes," she says.

"Yours rock too," I say gesturing to her Keds.

"Let's dive right into this. I want to put your skills to the test right now," she says, then turns to the audience. "I have a surprise for The Fashion Hound. She didn't know about this in advance, but she's going to teach us what makes a good Trophy Husband."

She points back stage. "Bring out the boys," Helen says and then three good-looking men walk onto the stage. Helen stands up, gesturing for me to join her. "Since you're the world's leading expert on Trophy Husbands, we thought we would pick your brains about what makes a good candidate."

Okay, I didn't expect that. I thought this appearance would be more about the *why* of Trophy Husbands, and the chance to turn the tables. But I'm on TV, so I need to go with the flow.

"Just like picking a wine."

"Exactly. So you're the sommelier. I want you to evaluate these men and tell us how each one rates as a potential Trophy

Husband." She points to the first guy. "This is Troy. Say hello, Troy."

He follows her orders. "Hello," he says with a wave. Troy has thick brown hair, deep brown eyes, a nice tan, and high cheekbones.

"Troy is twenty-three, six-two, a tennis pro, and is fluent in French. What do you think?"

That he's nothing like Chris. That I have zero interest in him. That I don't want to appraise men as if they're livestock.

Instead, I stick with the original definition of a Trophy Husband and give my answer swiftly and immediately based on that criterion. "Height is perfect. I like that he's athletic. The job – tennis pro – kind of sounds like you're probably not into working very hard, *which* is a good thing for a kept man, but at least you have a skill to keep you busy. And I have to say the French is a nice touch. Very nice."

I tell myself this is like speed dating, and it'll be over soon.

"Next, we have Ethan." Helen moves to the guy in the middle. Ethan has straight brown hair, streaked with blond highlights. His hair hangs a little shaggily across his forehead, covering his blue eyes a bit, until he sweeps it back. His hair reminds me of Chris, but I force myself to push the thought of him away for now. "Ethan is twenty-one, six feet tall, an amateur skateboarder, and knows how to cook Indian food."

"I *love* Indian food, so that is a big plus. But the skater part worries me. Skaters can be slackers, and while I don't need you to work, I do need you to not be a complete bum."

Helen continues with the final man. "Here is Javier." Javier is a little shorter, in good shape, with close-cropped black hair and warm hazel eyes. "He is five-eleven, hails from Brazil, works as a lifeguard, and loves to give footrubs."

"Foot rubs are huge, Helen. Any Trophy Husband worth his salt should be skilled in footrubs. And the international flare is a great touch. I can trot that out easily in social circles to impress people."

"So, right now, if you had to pick, who'd be the best Trophy Husband?"

"Troy," I say firmly. "Il parle francais."

"Voulez vous to you," Helen says. Then she dismisses the men and they disappear offstage. We head over to her couch. "Look at you, just sizing them up and slicing them down, just like that. So this Trophy Husband project is all about empowerment, alpha females, going against the grain."

"Two can play at the trophy spouse game, I say."

"So this is a crusade, a cause?"

"Exactly. But now I want other women to take up the mantle. We've been told for years to date older men, but we can snag younger men too. Much younger men."

Helen becomes more excited. "You're amassing followers, aren't you?"

"So many we should form an army."

Helen can't get enough of this. She slaps her palm on the arm of the couch. I take that as a cue to keep going. "I believe women can do what men can do. And we don't have to feel bad. We don't have to explain ourselves. We can just do it."

The audience loves this, they are enraptured. I am going to end this on a high note. No one will remember that I bowed out the same day. They will remember the message and a generation of women who come after me will collect Trophy Husbands and they will remember this moment when I led them to the promised land of equality.

"I can't imagine you've had any trouble finding takers though. So where do we stand in your quest? You've been dating JP and Craig and this guy Chris, but we never saw the video from that date. Are you really going to go through with this? Are you going to walk down the aisle?"

I open my mouth to answer, but no words come out.

Helen is a pro though and she ably fills in the silence with humor. "What I really want to say is can I help you pick out your dress? Maybe help you get a tiara for your hair, a little princess crown or something? And maybe we can schedule your wedding to the Trophy Husband winner to air on TV too?"

The prospect sounds horrifying, and it's as if there's a weed in my stomach, twisting its way around my insides, latching onto my organs. A few hours ago, I thought the cause still mattered. I thought the point was worth making. But despite the new threats from Todd, the lying is gnawing away at me, and I don't want to feel consumed by revenge anymore. If he's going to go after my business, I'll have to deal. That's what lawyers are for and my friend is married to the best of them. I'll get through whatever mud Todd slings my way just as I got through the break-up – with a little help from my friends.

A million thoughts race through my mind in this instant, a million voices. Chris saying 'When this point is no longer important to you, that's when you should call me again.' I hear Andy's words: 'He doesn't care what you do. He doesn't care if you prove him wrong. I doubt Amber cares either.' I hear Hayden's daughter: 'I think you should find a nice boy. I want you to be happy. I want you to find your sailboat in the moonlight.' And my sister Julia: ' When I find someone I can actually talk to that's when I'll know I've found the one.' The voices grow stronger, louder, like a Greek chorus, echoing in my ears.

And that chorus guides me on to this moment. To this truth: there's no more getting even, just living my life, moving on.

Helen is staring at me, and I can tell she's getting ticked that I'm no longer rattling off quips and snark. This is TV, after all, and she doesn't want any dead time. I don't want to let her down. I want to give her something good. And I realize this is the perfect way for me to move on. To drop the anger, to say goodbye to getting even, and to step into my future.

"Actually Helen, I have a confession to make."

She rubs her hands together. She's glad this segment may be back on track. "Do tell."

I take a deep breath. "The contest is over."

"Over?"

I nod. "Yes, I made the decision this weekend, and I'm announcing it now for the first time. It's over because I don't want a Trophy Husband. It's over because I don't want to marry a younger man just to get even. It's over because no contest, no boy toy, no hot young thing will ever change the fact that my ex-fiancé ditched me for another woman. But most of all, and most important, it's over because I met someone along the way, and he's the one I want. And there's one more thing I want to say, and I hope you don't mind me saying this on your show." I look to her as a flock of nerves descends on me, beating their wings. But I have to live with this vulnerability. I have to be okay with it. I think I am.

Helen is surprised with the curveball, but she's not a national TV show host for nothing. "As long as you don't swear on my show."

"I didn't just meet someone. I fell for him. I fell in love with him. I couldn't help it, and he swept me away. That's what happened. That's how I feel. Like magic, and music, and everything the love songs promise. The kind where there's no question about it, and it can't be any other way. And that's why there will be no Trophy Husband, because if he still wants me like I want him then I'm here to say that I'm much happier with a boyfriend than I could ever be with making a point."

188

Her lips quirk up, as if she's assessing me. But then she looks to the studio audience. "What do you think?"

They clap and they cheer, and soon there's a collective sort of "aww" coming from the crowd.

Helen pumps her fist and nods appreciatively at me. "I love this woman! She had the crap kicked out of her by love, and she got up on the horse and rode again. Forget revenge fantasies. You are the poster child for taking a chance again at love."

I like that title better. A lot better.

Chapter Nineteen

I wait in the lobby for Tristan. I keep checking my phone, but Chris won't have called because he hasn't seen the show yet. It won't air until this afternoon. Even though all my instincts tell me to run over to his apartment, jump into his arms and smother him in kisses, the reality is I am in a holding pattern for hours. It's as if I'm flying cross-country, sans phone, sans connection to the world, until later today.

Soon, Tristan reappears with a thumb drive. He hands it to me with a flourish then kisses my cheek. "In all its technicolor glory. Now, don't post it until four-thirty. That's when the segment will have run live. You can post the clip anytime after."

"Promise."

"You are a brave woman, and I hope that man knows he's damn lucky to have you."

"I'm damn lucky if he'll still have me."

Tristan gives me a confident wave. Then he leans in to whisper. "And if you met any men along the way who bat for my team, you just send them my way."

"You know, I might actually know someone for you. Take a picture with me."

He drapes an arm over my shoulder and smiles for the camera as I turn my phone around to capture us. Then I take down Tristan's number.

* * *

Andy has never looked happier than when he shoots today's video. He high-fives me when it's over. "I cannot wait to edit that clip in. I'm proud of you."

"Thank you. Her show airs in about thirty minutes, so we can run when my segment is over. But let me know the second it's live, okay?"

"I will."

"Oh, and what do you think about this guy?"

I tap the photos on my phone and show Andy the one I shot a little while ago. He peers at the screen. "He's not bad," Andy says, and there's a flirty sound in his voice. My Andy is back. My Andy helped bring me back.

"He's single."

"Then he's really not bad."

"He lives in San Francisco. He has a good job."

"You really can't resist engineering things, can you?"

"No," I say with a laugh. "Do you want me to set you up?"

"Sure."

Then he waves and drives off.

* * *

I brace myself when Hayden bangs on my door. I answer it, hunching my shoulders forward, fully prepared for her to launch a verbal attack of *why did I have to learn this on TV* and *how could you keep this from me?*

But she's the first to congratulate me. "I heard the news. You sneaky bitch! Why didn't you tell me?"

"I don't know," I say, but I'm smiling. "I guess I was scared."

"I am pretty frightening."

"I didn't want to let you down."

"I will be seriously let down if you don't tell me everything now."

So we move from my doorway and sit on the steps, and her eyes grow wider at the Fish Out of Water Studios part, they become saucers when I tell her about Qbert, and then she shrieks as I recount the news of my on-air admission.

"Wow," she says, with something like awe in her voice. "I feel like that has the making of some crazy romance novel."

"Oh, stop it with you and your romance novels."

"No seriously. The best ones have these crazy plots, and earth-shattering orgasms, and then some big gesture like confessing your love on a billboard, and then the happily ever after."

"I'm hoping for the latter. But I feel terrible. You guys worked so hard to help me find a Trophy Husband and I just bailed on it."

"We cheered you on because we thought it would make you happy. Because we thought you'd be able to move on."

"So you're not mad at me for dropping the contest?"

"I told you, McKenna – I've always wanted you to be happy. Whether you're happy with a guy, without a guy, with an older guy, with a younger guy, even if you decided to go girl on me. All I want is for you to be happy. I could never be mad. Especially because you are crazy and insane and you make us do things we haven't done since college."

"But now it's all over."

"We may have to resort to egging people's home or toilet papering trees."

"Such low-brow pranks."

"I am confident with enough time you will devise something new."

"And I went out with him too the night of our girls night out."

"You broke the golden rule of a girls night out," she says admonishing me. Then she rolls her eyes. "Besides, I figured you were talking to someone you liked that night. Even though I'm so totally bothered and completely annoyed that my best friend has fucking fallen in love."

* * *

But I don't hear from Chris all through the evening. I don't hear from him even after I forward him today's episode of The Fashion Hound. I don't hear from him as I walk Ms. Pac-Man, as I give her dinner, as I heat up pasta for myself. As each minute of radio silence from him passes, I want to rewind the day, to do it over, to do something, anything, differently.

I brace myself for the inevitable – for more silence as I read through emails, and comments and posts from viewers of *The Fashion Hound*. Most of them are thrilled, they love love, and stories of love, and big showy declarations, and they're dying to know what Chris said.

But naturally with my luck, my efforts fell on deaf ears, and I'm back where I started. Alone, with a six-pack of Diet Coke and a bad attitude for company. I open the fridge and crack open a can when my phone rings. I feel that burst of hope that it might be him, then the fear that I'll be disappointed.

When I grab it from the table, I see his name, and I know that at the very least I'll have an answer.

"Hello?" I ask nervously as I put the can down on the table.

He doesn't respond. Instead, I hear the notes of a song I know so well, a song I want to live in, a song I want to feel inside and out. It used to be torture. Now it feels like joy, and you'd need industrial strength cleaner to wipe the ridiculous grin off my face. Then I realize where the song is coming from. Outside my window.

I drop my phone, run down the stairs, my dog following close behind, and open the door. He's here. At my house. On my steps. Looking casual and cool in cargo shorts and an orange faded tee-shirt that fits him well as he holds his phone up high and plays my favorite song. To me. For me. I want to hug him. I want to kiss him. I want to be with him in every way. Because he's here. He found me. He came to me. I'm so damn happy right now I could power a rocket to Jupiter and back.

"So you really like this guy, huh?"

"Totally."

"I'm pretty sure he's crazy in love with you too."

"I was about to chew off my leg if I didn't hear from you."

He laughs. "I would have called sooner, I swear. I was in the studio all evening and there's no cell reception, so I didn't see your email til just now. Then I watched your show, and –" he stops, and gestures to the dog, who's wagging her tail. "I think she wants me to come inside."

"I want you to come inside."

We don't make it to my bedroom. I place my hands on his cheeks and start kissing him on the stairs the second I shut the door. He responds fiercely and we are all lips and tongue and teeth crashing into each other in an anthemic song of kissing, a big epic tune of music, and passion, and hope. Of falling in love again. Of letting go and starting over. He lifts me up and I wrap my legs around his waist, and he carries me up the steps, and lays me down on the couch.

He looks at me, appraising me, and I feel so vulnerable, but so right about this, about him, about us, as he trails his hand down my bare leg. I sigh, as he kisses my ankle, then makes his way to my calf, stopping to plant a tender, but hot kiss behind my knee, and soon I am wriggling, and wanting, and needing so desperately to feel him.

"I am so incredibly in love with you, McKenna. You have no idea how awesome it was to watch that segment. It was the coolest thing ever because I totally feel the same. You are everything I have ever wanted in a chick, and I'm so glad you're mine."

I am flying high right now. "I am totally madly in love with you, Chris," I say, just because I can. Then, in a lower voice, I breathe out his name. "*Chris*." I don't have to ask. He knows it's time. He knows I'm ready.

He strips off my skirt and I pull off my top, not caring where they wind up.

His hand makes it way from my waist up to my hair again. I move closer to kiss him and find myself sighing when my lips meet his again, in a new kiss, a slower kiss than the one by the door, the kind of kiss that's a promise of what's to come. He tastes so good, these sweet soft lips of his. I touch the soft fabric of his tee-shirt and my right hand drifts down to his abdomen, to the waistband of his shorts. I feel his hands exploring too, as he reaches around to my back, unsnapping my bra. He tosses my bra to the side of the coffee table and places his hands on my breasts.

"Mmm, these are great," he says, like a kid in a candy store.

"They're real, you know," I say, a little boastfully.

"Oh, I know. And I like it that way." He plays with them more, cupping them, licking them, kneading them, pretty much unable to take his hands off of them. "Ever since I met you I have wanted to get your shirt off."

"Don't take this the the wrong way, but I should tell you I have felt the same about getting your shirt off." Then I lift his shirt up and over his head. I run my hands across his arms, his chest, his trim waistline with just the right amount of cut to his belly. I trace the outline of his abs with my fingers. He's firm and toned and I want to keep running my fingers across him, sort of like when you can't stop touching a rabbit's coat, and the sensation, the feeling, the touch draws you back for more. Then I make my way down to his boxer briefs.

"I'm going to need to take these off."

"Be my guest," he says as I strip off his underwear. He's naked next to me, reaching for my panties, taking them off swiftly too.

"I hope you have a condom because I don't," I say.

"I had a feeling we might need one," he says and reaches for his wallet inside his shorts, and I'm so glad he had the foresight to bring one, because I can't wait a moment longer. He rolls it on as I watch him. God, he's beautiful, all of him, every inch of him, and he's here with me. He wants to be with me, and he's so fucking sexy as he prepares to enter me. I place my hands on his shoulders, but then he shifts so he's on his back and he moves me on top of him.

"I have a feeling you like to be on top."

"However did you know?"

"Just a wild guess."

I lower myself onto him. I draw a sharp intake of breath, close my eyes and let the feeling of him filling me up take over me. Then I open my eyes again and look down at him. His hands are on my hips and he moves slowly inside me. It's a deliciously lazy kind of rhythm, in and out, long and leisurely strokes that reach every part of me, and intoxicate me with the most wonderful drug of him. Of Chris. Of being in love. As he moves in me, sparks fly through my whole body, racing through my blood, through my veins. I close my eyes, because reality is too intense right now to have to see it. I just want to feel right now. So I lean down to kiss him and he draws me against him, my breasts pressing into his chest. "I have to tell you, Chris. It takes me a long time. A really long time."

196

"I don't have anyplace to be," he whispers. "Other than with this girl I'm crazy in love with."

So I make love to my one-time business partner, my erstwhile partner in crime. He is none of those. Right now, he's here with me, just me, as I touch his strong chest, then as my hands fumble in his soft hair that I love like crazy. There is no hidden agenda as I linger on the feeling of him all the way inside me. There is no game as he moves me up and down on him, holding me close, holding me near.

He brushes a strand of hair away from my face, and touches my cheek, then my neck in a gesture that floods me with so many emotions that scare the hell out of me, but feel so good too. The way he holds my hips as he drives into me is as consuming as it is tender, making me tremble, because we are so connected, so in tune that I know now what *perfect* means. This is perfect with him. This is more than perfect.

He is everything I could ever want, and he's mine.

I've never cried during sex, and I hope I never do. But in this moment, I am overwhelmed with the intensity of all that I feel for him. I want as much of him as I can have, and he fills me so completely as I quicken the pace, moving in synch with him, in a delicious sort of rhythm that builds as he drives me higher, and my belly tightens and I draw in a deep breath, and then he brings me there.

It's a waterfall, crashing over me, in my body, and in my heart, and so I bury my face in his neck, as I say his name louder, and my voice nearly breaks, and I hope he knows it's because his name is the only one I ever want tumbling forth from my lips.

I shudder, and fall onto his chest, and then he rocks into me, saying my name many times too, then kissing me softly and holding me close, as I think of music, and lyrics, and sailboats in the moonlight.

Chapter Twenty

A week later, I'm walking home from the coffee shop when I run into Amber on her way to her gymnastics class. I don't have anything to say to her, but I don't want to avoid her either. I won't let her have that much power in my life.

So instead of slinging a snide remark, I suck in all my pride, and say, "Hi Amber."

Without agenda, without anger, without that jealousy that encased me for the last year.

"Hi McKenna. I've been meaning to reach out to you."

I stay strong. Whatever she has to say, whatever they will throw my way, I'll manage. I wait for her.

"I wanted to let you know that I had no idea what Todd was up to with the business buyout bullshit. But as soon as I heard last night, I sat him down and told him it was not okay. I told him to back off and stop threatening you with legal battles."

"You did? You said that?"

"Yes. I made it clear that he was not going to operate our family that way. We make our own money. We don't try to take money that belongs to other people. And The Fashion Hound is yours, and yours alone. So he spoke to his lawyer this morning to let him know he won't need his services."

A brittle piece of my heart softens. I'm not going to be friends with Amber, we're not about to get mani-pedis together, but I respect her for this.

"Thank you, Amber. Thank you for that."

"I better get to class."

"Happy cartwheeling," I say, and I mean it.

I walk the last few blocks to my house and am surprised to find two delivery men and a large truck waiting outside my steps.

"You McKenna Bell?"

I nod. "We have a delivery for you."

"Evidently. What is it?"

But the guy doesn't answer. Instead, he returns to the truck, and wheels a dolly down the ramp. When he's halfway down I see what's on the dolly.

My very own Qbert. An arcade Qbert.

"Oh my god!" I clap my hand to my mouth and I jump in excitement.

"Built it myself."

I turn around and there's Chris walking around from the front of the truck.

"You did?"

"I had a feeling you might like your own."

Fifteen minutes later, the delivery guys are gone, and there's a gorgeous new game in my living room.

"It's one hundred percent authentic," Chris says, and then hands me a bag of quarters. "No freebies. You gotta pay this beast every time."

My eyes light up and I reach for a quarter. "I want to play now."

"There's one thing I should let you know, though. I tested it out first. Just to make sure it worked. So you'll have to beat my high score."

He taps the screen and shows me his score. It's insanely high. I pretend to punch him. "Chris! That's too high. It'll take me forever to beat your score."

"We can just christen the game instead then."

Epilogue

Two Months Later

The cabs honk, and the traffic roars, and everywhere there are people, bustling and coming and going. Chris holds my hand as we weave through streams of New Yorkers and tourists. I'm wearing a black linen dress with cartoonish dog prints smattered across the fabric, and a flouncy skirt that shows off a hot pink petticoat underneath. It's totally retro and rockabilly, and I love it. So does Chris, who looks sharp in jeans and a button-down shirt as he guides us to the stage door.

He knocks and the stage manager opens the door shortly.

"Hi. You are?"

"Chris McCormick. Here to see my sister Jill."

The stage manager glances at a list in her hand, taps it once to confirm, and then shows us into the theater, escorting us through narrow hallways that whisper stories of the past, of plays and productions and big, brassy musicals that this jewel of Broadway has seen over the years. Down a well-worn red carpeted hallway to a dressing room, and the stage manager knocks. We are early. Curtain is in one hour. But it's opening night at Chris' sister's show, and she said she wanted to see him beforehand.

She opens the door and flashes a huge smile then jumps into his arms.

"Hey, little sis."

"Hey, big pain in the ass."

"I see you haven't changed."

"I can still beat you up."

"You so wish you could."

Then she turns to me, and she's gorgeous, with beautiful blond hair pinned up on her head, and heavy stage makeup that accentuates strong cheekbones and dark eyes. She's wearing a white tee-shirt splotched with paint stains, and a pair of loose jeans. I'm not sure if they're her costume, or just casual backstage clothes.

"I can't believe I'm finally meeting you. You're even hotter in person."

I blush. "Stop that."

"No, seriously. I can't believe my brother snagged a total babe. How did you trick her, Chris?" she says to her brother, and I love the back-and-forth banter. Then she turns to me, and wraps me in a hug. She lowers her voice and whispers just to me. "I'm so glad he found you. He's mad about you."

"The feeling is completely mutual."

"So I'm sure you guys want to see the stage before the show starts," Jill says, then guides us out of the dressing room, down the hallway, past other actors and stagehands who she says hello to. Then to the wings, and onto the stage.

The set is breathtaking in its minimalist glory, and I gasp. "It's amazing," I say, then we turn around and take in all the empty seats in the theater, seats that will soon be filled up with patrons here on opening night of *Crash the Moon*.

Jill smacks her forehead. "I forgot something in my dressing room. I'll be right back."

Then it's just Chris and me on an empty stage in a Broadway theater.

I turn to him and am shocked to see him down on one knee.

"I'm pretty sure they want to get their stage back soon, so I'm seizing this moment."

He looks so earnest, so full of hope, as he reaches into his pocket and takes out a dark velvet box. His nervous fingers fumble at the opening, and his light brown hair falls across his forehead. I can already feel my throat hitching and tears welling, as he takes out a stunning diamond in a vintage style cut that couldn't be more perfect for me.

"When we first met, I thought you were a babe. Then I got to know you and I thought you were the coolest chick ever. And it all started with you wanting me to pretend to be trying out to be your Trophy Husband. So what I really want now is not to be your Trophy Husband, but just to be your husband."

"Yes," I say, and my voice breaks, and the tears come, and I'm shaking as he slides a ring onto my finger because I am overjoyed.

"Okay, let's clear the stage now."

* * *

I can't stop looking at my ring. I don't think I will ever stop looking at it. The theater fills, and soon the overture begins, and I spread open the Playbill and point to his sister's name.

"Look. There's your sister. Look at the role she's playing."

"I know. It's amazing, isn't it?"

"Totally," I say. "Hey, do I have to take your name? Because McKenna McCormick would be pretty silly."

"Take my name or don't take my name. All I care about is that you're mine forever. For always."

"I am."

Then the music swells, and the sound of the orchestra fills the theater, and I hold hands with my favorite person in the world as the musical begins.

Acknowledgements

First and foremost, a ginormous thanks to the readers. Without you, well, this book would not have been possible. I am so so so grateful for your support, your notes, your tweets, your messages, and most of all your passion for romance, especially the kind I write. I love hearing from you, and I am grateful for each and every one of you. Romance readers are THE BEST - a vocal and awesome crew and I want to hug all of you.

Writing is such a solitary act, but editing and publishing are not. I am honored and humbled to have amazing critique partners like Cyn, Summer Stone, Simone Noelle, Kelli and CS. My business advisor, Simone, is my go-to gal every day, and I would not be on this indie journey if she hadn't encouraged me and guided me. THANK YOU, Simone. Then there is my biggest advocate, Michelle, who somehow manages to make sense of the insanity of our plans, and does it with passion, intensity and a gung-ho attitude. I adore the indie writing community and can not imagine navigating it without my indie BFF Monica Murphy. That indie family now also includes the amazingly awesome authors Kristen Proby, Kendall Ryan, Emma Hart, Lexi Ryan, Melody Grace and Paige Edward. Big thanks to Kristen and Kendall for the fabulous blurbs!

A special thanks to Kelly Simmons at Inkslinger PR for her focus, dedication and use of words like "lickable" to refer to stock photos. And for believing in this book.

Sarah Hansen at Okay Creations blew this cover out of the water with her work. Holy hotness! You are a cover wizard, Sarah! Giselle at Xpresso organized an amazing cover reveal. Thank you, Giselle!

The indie world thrives on word of mouth, Goodreads, social media and the amazing bloggers who bring so much passion to books. I am indebted for the support of amazing bloggers including Cara at Book Whores Obsession, Kari at Sub Club, Taryn at My Secret Romance, Angie at Angie's Dreamy Reads, Becky at Reality Bites, Sugar and Spice Book Reviews, My Fictional Boyfriend, Denise and Nic at Flirty Dirty, Tammy & Kim Reviews, Romance Addict, Jessica and Lyndsay at Little Black Book Blog, Christine at Shh…Mom's Reading, and more.

And most of all a big thanks to my family. I love you all so so so much.

Sneak Peek at **Playing With My Heart**

Tentatively Slated for an August release

Dear Readers: After reading *Caught Up In Us*, many of you asked when I would tell Jill's story. Likewise, after reading *Pretending He's Mine*, where Jill also plays a key role, many readers inquired as to when they'd get her story. I'm thrilled to let you know I'm busy writing *Playing With My Heart* and am aiming for a summer release. To whet your appetite, here's the first chapter. (Note: This is unedited and may change in the final version.)

Xoxo

Lauren

Playing With My Heart
Chapter One

Davis

The moment this girl steps on stage to sing her solo, I know - without a shadow of a doubt - that she's our Ava. Her voice gives me chills. She starts small, as the song calls for, in a trembling kind of tone, and then through each verse her voice strengthens, matching the lyrics, the tone of the song, the story the music is telling: a girl who was all alone, but who had to find her own way to her dream, and found it through pain and patience and heartache.

When she reaches the chorus, her voice is all I feel, and it's got arms and fingertips that stretch from the center of the stage, all the way around the theater to the balcony. A voice that surrounds you, and mesmerizes you with color and heat and tremulous tenderness.

The voice has layers and hurt all in one, and so does this actress, her face, the way she wrings the emotion from the words.

I have goosebumps all over, as I rest my elbows on my thighs, my hands clasped together, seeing only her. I want to hold onto this moment, this feeling, because it comes around so rarely. Usually, it's in London when I see a huge star perform, or sometimes it's when I go to Lincoln Center for a one-night only performance of a legend. So few and far between, I can count them on one hand, being blown away by a new talent. By someone I could cast in a new Frederick Stillman musical, so she'd make her New York theater debut, and I'd be the director who discovered the next big Broadway star.

This girl is It. She'll haul home Tonys over the years, she'll lure in TV deals, and cut CDs, and the denizens of theater the world over will adore her.

I can feel it in my bones. She's my lead. She's going to bring down the house. She's going to make the audience cry and soar, and then get on their feet for the loudest, biggest standing ovation.

When she finishes, I nearly can't help myself. I want to stand up, shake her hand, and tell her she's been cast. But I can't. The executive producer and composer can veto me, though I have no intention of letting that happen. I have never been more sure of a casting choice than I am now.

Even so, I restrain myself. "Thank you so much. Now, the scene and song with Mr. Carlson."

Patrick Carlson, who was cast long ago as the lead in *Crash the Moon* jumps up from the red upholstered chair next to me. He's here at the final auditions, along with Don Kraftig, the producer, and with Mr. Stillman himself.

Frederick Stillman, the most revered composer in the last quarter century, who's collected armfuls of awards for best musical. Actors fall all over themselves to star in his shows, directors fawn at his feet.

I would have fawned to land this gig, but I didn't have to.

I've won three Tonys, one Oscar, and my Broadway shows have all returned on their investors' dollars. I directed a film too – that's how I nabbed that golden statuette. So Stillman called me. Called my cell one fine afternoon six months ago, and told me he was offering the directing job to me, only me, and to no one but me.

I said yes on the spot.

Now I want to say yes to this girl.

Jill

My twenty-two years on earth have led me to this moment.

Every singing lesson I ever took.

Every acting class I ever went to.

Every play I read, every song I heard, every emotion I called forth from deep inside for every part I've ever played before.

Here. Now. Today.

But really, more than anything, the fact that I finished five marathons matters most right now. Because of that, I have the training, the perseverance, and the composure to not freak the fuck out when I walk across the floorboards of the St. James theater to join Patrick Carlson on stage. I can barely see the powers-that-be because the seats are shrouded in darkness, and the lights are on the stage. But I can make out the silhouette of the director in the second row, along with the producer, and the God I bow down to – Frederick Stillman himself, who wrote this anthemic musical, which I fell in love with. I would enter the Hunger Games for a chance to perform in something he's created, but fortunately all I have to do is nail an audition with Patrick Carlson.

So, as if I'm running with the kind of focus I need for 26 miles – blinders on, nothing but blinders – I ignore the fact that Patrick Carlson is the most beautiful man I've ever seen, that his honey blond hair looks thick and soft and that his light brown eyes are so inviting I want to swim in them.

Okay, maybe not his eyes. Because. Ew. Creepy.

But they are magnetic, and they draw me in, as if they have their own lifeforce.

Wait. Can eyes have a lifeforce? Or are they more like tractor beams? Or magnets?

Actually, neither image will help me now, so I implement *The Jill McCormick Ran Five Marathons Brainsweep*, and I can hear the silent *boop-beep-bop* of futuristic sounding computer keys silencing these silly thoughts, as I forget that his talent alone inspired me in high school. I abandon the memories of all the times I skipped class in college to second act matinees of *Rent* to watch him play Roger, or *Wicked* to see him as Fyero.

I am no longer Jill, aspiring New York actress auditioning for her first Broadway role, and he is not Patrick, the man who exudes talent and charisma every second he's on stage.

He's Paolo and he's my teacher. Right now I am Ava, a young painter without a family, and he's a mercurial and captivating artist. I face the audience – nearly two thousand empty seats and only a few occupied ones, the spotlights from above shining brightly, as he steps behind me.

He says not a word. Instead, he breathes out, "hmmm," as he places his hands on my arms, as if he's considering me, then runs his palms sensuously from my wrists to my shoulders.

"You must let go, Ava. You try too hard to make your paintings perfect. You need to make them you."

I nod, breathless, speechless, because this man I've admired, looked up to, is touching me. My art teacher, and the renowned painter. He brushes my hair away from my neck, and I lean my head to the side, letting him trace the vein in my neck with his finger. Then, as if I've just remembered that I'm a good girl, that I don't do this, won't do this, can't do this, I pull away.

Because I am, shockingly – me – a good girl.

"I am only here to learn."

He narrows his eyes at me. "I am teaching you."

Ava wants to correct him, to tell him he's not, that he's crossing lines, even though the crossing of them feels good to this girl who's felt far too much of the not-good in life for far too long. But Ava's not ready yet for this. Soon, but not yet, so she – me, because I'm her, completely and utterly subsumed by her – wheels on him, fire in her eyes, then lashes out with the first sung lines in a heated duet.

"You don't have permission to lay your hands on me."

He plays the gentleman, giving a gesture of surrender. "Forgive me then, I only touch you as your teacher," he sings softly, but powerfully in that baritone that could melt igloos.

"That's not teaching."

"Then find you own way to paint, child."

And he starts to walk off.

Ava huffs, crosses her arms, looks away, and sings roughly of all the ways this man makes her crazy. He tells her how her brushstrokes are too controlled, her head is too much in the way, she needs to throw her body into the act of painting. And I hate it, and him, because he feels like the one thing that stands between true creativity and me.

I sing an angry lament, a furious plea to the universe to send me elsewhere. But yet, there is no place else for me, nowhere to go. I've been left all alone, and all I have is my art, and he's the only one who can make it better.

Make me better.

So I chase him before he leaves the empty classroom, and leaves me all alone. Ava detests aloneness, even though it's the thing she knows best. He's nearly off-stage, and I grab his shirt, and he gives me this look – satisfaction and curiosity.

"I see you've changed your mind…"

My shoulders fall in resignation of Ava's reality. I will only succeed with him. "I need you, Professor Paolo."

"Don't call me professor."

"What should I call you?"

"You can call me anytime."

And then he casually runs a strand of my hair in his fingers and lets it fall. I grab him, bestowing a hard, wet kiss on his lips.

Patrick's lips. Paolo's lips.

Oh god. He tastes fucking divine. Paolo. Patrick. My teacher. The actor I idolize. They all collide at once – reality, make believe, years of crushing, a moment of pretending. I don't know if the way I feel right now comes from me or from Ava, but all I know is – without even opening my eyes, without even hearing 'end scene' – we have a crazy kind of chemistry that can't be faked.

Then I break the kiss and run offstage where I slam into Alexis Carbone, all bleached blond, bosom, and pipes like nobody's business.

I don't stand a chance.

Coming Next

Keep your eye out for my first books with Entangled Publishing this fall!

In September: A sexy Halloween novella starring a scorchingly-hot firefighter who melts hearts and panties...

In October: THE BREAK-UP ALBUM, a story of a rock star who has to choose between love and music...

Available for pre-order soon...

Sneak Peek of **The Impact of You**
by Kendall Ryan and **Unbreak Me** by Lexi Ryan

Dear Readers: I am thrilled to share a sneak peek of two New Adult romances I can't wait to read! The first is *The Impact of You* from Kendall Ryan, releasing June 11, and the second is *Unbreak Me* by Lexi Ryan, releasing May 27. (Note: These are unedited and may change in the final version.) Look for these books and check them out in the coming weeks!

Xoxo

Lauren

The Impact of You by Kendall Ryan,
New York Times and USA Today Bestselling author

About the book…

Needing an escape from her past, Avery chooses a college where no one knows her. Keeping a low profile was the plan, falling for the intense frat boy, Jase wasn't. Yet she can't deny how alive she feels when he's near. Even as common sense implores her to stay away, her body begs her to get closer. Jase, numb from his own family drama, has grown bored with weekends fueled by nameless girls and countless bottles when he meets Avery. Helping her cope with her past is better than dealing with the bullshit his own life's served up. Determined to drive away the painful secret she's guarding, he appoints himself her life coach, and challenges her to new experiences. Getting close to her and being the one to make her smile are simply perks of the job. But when Avery's past boldly saunters in, refusing to be forgotten, can Jase live with the truth about the girl he's fallen for?

Excerpt from **The Impact of You...**

"Thanks." I take my coffee and try a sip. Jase is still watching me, a lopsided grin across his lips. "What?"

He chuckles softly, the deep timber of his voice raking over me, then folds his hands on the table in front of him. "Fine, I'll do it."

"Do what?"

He smirks. "I see no other choice than to become your tutor."

This time I'm the one laughing. "You want to be my human sexuality tutor? That's original. And not douchey at all."

Jase's determined gaze meets mine. "As tempting as that offer is – and there's so much I could teach you – no. I meant I could tutor you at...life."

"Gee thanks. Why don't you just admit you think I'm a loser with no life and get on with it."

"I didn't say loser. Lost...probably. Not having as much fun as you should be...definitely."

"Rip the Band-Aid off why don't you."

Jase settles back against his seat, sliding his cup of coffee toward him in the process. "Just calling it like I see it, babe."

He's too relaxed, too smug. I want to lash out irrationally and say something to wipe that cocky smile from his face. Instead, I pull in a deep breath and reflect on his observation of me. I'm sitting stick-straight in my seat, my stack of textbooks is neatly lined up in front of me, and each time Jase has seen me – first at the party, then behind the dumpster – I've been hiding. I wish I could tell him those were isolated incidents, that I'm not really like that, but sadly I am. I realize with a flash of clarity, Jase is right. And suddenly I want more.

I lean toward him on my elbows, weighing his offer. "So how would this life-coaching work exactly...I'm not saying I'm interested, but if I was..."

"We'd need to begin spending more time together for starters."

I nod, listening intently. I'm thankful he doesn't know my heart just kicked into overdrive at his words. "What else?"

Jase abandons his casual posture, leaning in towards me across the table, his brilliant blue eyes piercing mine with intensity. "I'll issue you challenges as I see fit. You'd have to trust me."

I fold my arms across my chest. "I'm not running through campus naked or dropping acid or anything weird like that."

"I wouldn't ask you to do anything you're not ready for." His voice is calm and sure. I can't believe I'm considering this, but I am.

"Why would you want to do all this...I'm not a project."

"I didn't say you were. Let's just say I could use the distraction right now."

I know my expression gives me away. I'm beyond confused about what's happening between us and powerless to stop it.

He brushes his index finger over the crease in my forehead. "Hey, relax," his voice is just a whisper. "You're thinking too hard. I'm not going to pry about your past unless you want me to."

I shake my head, my heart thumping wildly.

Jase's thumb caresses my cheek before he lets his hand fall away. "You'll let me know if there's someone's ass I should kick, though, right?"

I would have giggled at this, had it not been for the intensity radiating from Jase. "No. I made my own choices."

He's silent while he studies me –his blue eyes looking for answers. Answers I can't possibly give him.

"You were young, too trusting, fell for the wrong guy..."

I clear my throat. "Something like that."

He reaches for my hand and gives it a squeeze. "Hey, it's okay."

I manage a nod, arranging my mouth in a smile. If he knew the truth, he wouldn't be sitting here, being so kind to me. My heart is thudding against my ribcage. "This tutoring thing...When do we start?"

He glances at his naked wrist. "Now would be nice."

I roll my eyes to avoid chuckling at him. "Fine. What's my first *assignment*?"

* * *

Unbreak Me by Lexi Ryan,
New York Times and USA Today Bestselling Author

About the book...

"If you're broken, I'll fix you..."

I'm only twenty-one and already damaged goods. A slut. A failure. A disappointment to my picture-perfect family as long as I can remember. I called off my wedding to William Bailey, the only man who thought I was worth fixing. A year later and he's marrying my sister. Unless I ask him not to... "If you shatter, I'll find you..." But now there's Asher Logan, a broken man who sees the fractures in my façade and doesn't want to fix me at all. Asher wants me to stop hiding, to stop pretending. Asher wants to break down my walls. But that means letting him see my ugly secrets and forgiving him for his. With my past weighing down on me, do I want the man who holds me together or the man who gives me permission to break?

Excerpt from **Unbreak Me....**

Technically, I am trespassing. *Technically*, trespassing is not part of the New Me plan. But it hardly feels like trespassing to use the neighbor's gorgeous, well-maintained pool when a) I've been doing it since I was sixteen, and b) the rich dude who owns the place is never around. I like to think I'm doing him a favor. He must spend a crap ton of money to maintain this place, but he doesn't get any use out of it because he's always away at his house in Vale or wherever. It would be wasteful for me *not* to use it just because of some technicality.

I hoist myself over the gate and feel greedy anticipation at the sight and sound of the water. Surrounded by lush landscaping and featuring a cascade of water that circulates from hot tub to pool, the space is more water feature than swimming hole. I don't know Rich Dude, but he has excellent taste, and this little oasis is one of my favorite places on Earth.

I could have headed home after the reception, but I knew I wouldn't sleep tonight. I told my mom I wanted to stay over, and I waited until everyone was in bed before grabbing a robe and trekking across a couple acres of lush grass for a moonlight swim.

I'm no stranger to insomnia, but it's been worse since I returned home. In the silence of the night, there's too much room for my thoughts and they expand until they fill every corner of my mind. While I was away, I could be anyone I wanted to be, but in New Hope, everywhere I turn, someone's labeling me. When I was young, I was just *one of the Thompson girls*, but now the labels aren't so innocuous. *Black sheep. College dropout.*

Slut.

I drop the terry cloth robe from my shoulders and dive into the water completely nude. Most pools would be intolerably cold in Indiana before June, but the water circulating from the hot tub keeps the water comfortable from spring to fall. Even if it was cold, I'd still be here. Exercise is the only thing that calms my mind. Tonight, I'll swim laps to escape the demons.

Until last year, small town life was the only life I'd ever known, so I should be used to it, but you can be cut open a hundred times, and the slice of the blade still hurts.

I just never expected Will to be the one holding the knife.

Does he love her? Would he marry my sister out of spite?

Did he tell Krystal the truth about our canceled vows?

I turn and pull my limbs through the water, asking myself the question I've been avoiding for weeks. *Can I live here and watch Will and Krystal build a life together?*

I count out twenty-five laps. The rhythm of my breathing calms me. The water rushing over my skin salves my wounds. Finally, I rest forearms on the edge of the pool and gulp in air, focusing only on my breath and the water dripping from my face.

"Training for the Olympics?"

I snap my head up in surprise. In the soft glow of the moon, I can make out the bad boy from the reception. He stands in swim trunks three yards from me, a towel draped around his neck. I was right about the tats. He has some sort of starburst on his left peck, another circling his thick biceps.

"Sneak up on many girls?"

"Only the special ones." He drops the towel on a chair and dives into the water.

When he surfaces, my heart kicks up a beat. He's close. I could almost touch him if I reached out.

But even as my eyes tour his broad chest and sculpted shoulders, I back away. "What are you doing here?"

His eyebrow quirks. "I live here."

I snort. "No you don't." Then, when his expression remains stoic. "Shit. Really? You're Rich Dude?"

"Rich who?" He looks puzzled. And annoyed.

Giggles bubble up and slip past my lips. I've always pictured the owner of this property to be some white-haired old man with a cane and a monocle. Asher is so far off the mark, I can't help my laughter. "Shit. I'm sorry. I just…" I laugh more, and it feels damn good. My muscles are spent from my swim, my mind is calm, and laughing feels like a long-denied decadent treat.

"You haven't come to swim in a long time," he says softly.

That cuts my laughter short. "You watch me?" I want to feel violated by the idea. But the thought of *this* man watching me swim nude in his pool zips potent arousal through my veins.

Asher shakes his head, studying me. "My groundskeeper told me a young girl used to sneak in about once a week. I assume that was you?"

"Yeah," I say softly.

"Why'd you stop?"

"I left town for awhile."

"Looking for something?"

I shake my head. "Running away."

He nods, as if my answer is perfectly reasonable, and I get the sense that he doesn't just accept it, he *understands* it. His gaze settles on my mouth. When his eyes drop to the water and my bare breasts, his breath catches, and I feel that rush that comes from being desired, that false sense of worth I'm willing to be fooled by tonight. Suddenly, I want him to kiss me. Touch me. More.

I want to wash my loneliness away with the weight of a man's body on mine, to erase unwelcome memories with his mouth.

This man's body. This man's mouth.

"Sorry I had to disappear earlier." His voice is low, husky as watches me.

"I'd let you make it up to me," I murmur, closing the distance between us. I hesitate, but his gaze—hot, hungry, all over me—is all the invitation I need.

Contact

I love hearing from readers! You can find me on Twitter at LaurenBlakely3, or Facebook at LaurenBlakelyBooks, or online at LaurenBlakely.com. You can also email me at laurenblakelybooks@gmail.com.